SURVIVING
VALENTINE

Jessica Florence

Surviving Valentine

Copyright © 2013 Jessica Florence

ISBN-13:

978-0615884622

ISBN-10:

0615884628

TABLE OF CONTENTS

Surviving Valentine

Chapter 1

Scarlet

"Right hook. Left hook. Now press your thumbs into your attacker's eyes! Great job, everyone!" Watching these women successfully practice gouging their attacker's eyes was the highlight of my day. Being a teacher of self-defense has its moments. But when the women that come in finally feel confident that they can actually defend themselves is the best feeling in the world. Nothing like being able to stick it to the man!

The time had come when this class would soon be ending, and a new group of women who are insecure and non-confident would start their journey towards a new life. The ending of a class is always fun though, because we get to put all of our training to work. Our "attackers" get dressed up in protective gear from head to toe. We do real kicks to the groin, and real head-butts to disorient our attacker. I had to admit I found it a little amusing that most of our "attackers," the big, buff men of Norfolk, Virginia were being taken down by us little old females. Though it wasn't hard to find willing volunteers to help out with my classes. Norfolk, Virginia is a huge hot spot for military personnel, men who are always looking for ways to help civilians. Well it also helps that at the end of the week I buy all of my guys a round at the best sports bar in the area: Parkers. Luckily I have the hook up at Parkers since the owner also happens to be my best friend, Candace Parker. We met three years ago at a self-defense class, and have been kick-ass friends since then.

"Alright, everyone, you did great today! I look around this class and I see strong, confident women! I am so proud of you guys! Now next week we will be practicing thrusting the heel of our hands into our assailant's nose thus causing it to break. Practice your upward thrusts. Please not on another person yet! Have a great weekend, everyone!" All of the women gathered their things and left. Our lovely gentlemen started taking off their protective gear. While I was cleaning up so I'd be ready to leave, I heard "So, Scarlet, when are you finally going to give into your carnal feelings and go out with me?"

Sighing, I turned around to see Jimmy, a regular volunteer. Tall, blond, surfer type of guy. "Oh Jimmy baby, I don't think you would be able to handle these carnal feelings."

The sounds of "ooh burns" fill the room.

"Nice work, douche canoe," said a tall man. I mean, like gosh, he had to have been like 6'3. With blond hair cut short and gorgeous brown eyes.

Now that all that gear was off, WOW! Holy arms, Batman! I think his name is Ross. He signed up last minute to help with today's class. I get hit on a lot by the men that help out with class. Maybe it's the whole women in charge thing, but I felt safe around this guy.

"Now, boys, boys. You guys kicked ass today. I am just going to finish cleaning up and meet you guys at Parkers, say around six?" They all said "sounds good" in unison. That should give me time to shower and get decent.

As the boys leave, I swear his name was Ross approached me. Although he was one nice male specimen, I have been trying to stay away from male attention lately. "Hey, Scarlet, I just wanted to officially introduce myself. I know I kinda dropped in on short notice today. But I really love what you are doing here, and wanted to help in some way." Hm that's nice.

"I'm Ross Olsen, I'm a captain down at Station 8 in Chesapeake."Oh a firefighter, I should introduce him to Candace. She is obsessed with firefighters.

"My sister was attacked when she was in high school, and thanks to the self-defense class she took she got out of it without a scratch. So I really like helping out with these sort of things, you know?" Wow, this guy is an open book, huh?

"It's nice to officially meet you. I'm Scarlet Barnette, owner here at Scars. Thanks for letting us kick you around a bit." I smiled a huge cheesy smile. "Haha no problem, Scarlet." I get back to my cleaning so I can get out of here.

As I'm cleaning I catch a glimpse of myself in the mirror and gosh I was always such a frizzy mess after my classes. My chestnut, curly, brown hair was piled on top of my head with flyaway's going in every different direction. I still had a faint pink blush on my cheeks from the workout. But I will say my full lips always looked good after a workout, my green eyes look tired though. Well when you've lived twenty-four years like I have you would have a little depth in yours too. Any who, I needed to stop thinking and head home. I finished closing up the shop and I saw that Ross waited for me to finish so he could make sure I got to my car okay. Very gentlemanlike of him. I turned to him and spoke.

"Well I guess I will see you in a few for a round on me."

"Heck yeah, I've never been there before, but I hear it's awesome."

"Yeah it is pretty awesome; a lot of firemen, police officers, and military people hang out there. My friend who owns it does a lot of nice discounts for them; her brothers are in the navy and her dad who started the place was in the air force.

"So she really goes above and beyond for her people in uniform." "Sweet deal! Alright, see you later!"

I make my way to my beautiful 2009 Toyota 4Runner. I love my car. She rides so smoothly, and she can haul anything you throw at her. Plus, she looks pretty fierce if I do say so myself. Thankfully it's not a long drive to my house so it takes no time at all. As I came to a stop I glanced to the house to the left of mine. My one and only neighbor, Aunt Tara, as she made everyone call her, passed away two weeks ago. She was a firecracker that old lady.

At sixty-one you would think she would be sitting back knitting while hanging out with ten cats. Nope, not that old broad. She was widowed many years before. Since then she has been doing every extreme thing possible. I mean, routine sky diving trips, bungee jumping, clubbing, and avid surfing, anything you can think of. That old bat did it! Did she have ten cats? Nope, she had an eighty-five-pound, all black German shepherd named Roxy. Aunt

Tara was one of the most important people in my life, and now she was gone. She died on one of her routine sky diving trips; she had a heart attack. At least she died doing what she loved, right?

I loved her house, which is identical to mine. A two-story ranch style home with a wrap-around porch with red shutters. But the best part you ask? Oh I guess it's not that big of a deal, but our houses were on the beach! Yep, growing up in Asheville, North Carolina, mountains are your daily view. I have always wanted to live on the beach. One day my dream came true, and I loved it! I wondered what would happen to good ole Aunt Tara's house. She has a sister I am pretty sure lives somewhere in Virginia. Who knows, I guess. Hopefully I wouldn't have some creepy, fat, perv guy that liked to tan naked on the beach while listening to salsa music. Ew! I needed a shower after that thought.

I walked and opened my door only to be jumped on by that eighty-five-pound German shepherd I was talking about. Aunt Tara left me Roxy, the most awesome dog ever! She loved to give me hugs hello, and always tried to lick my face. But just the nose and mouth, nowhere else, it's so weird!

"Down, foxy Roxy!" My little nickname for her, because she is so foxy. She automatically sits and looks at me. Dinner time! I fixed Roxy's bowl with the goods and head towards my long awaited shower. I swear a nice hot shower could turn any day into a good day. It just washes away all the bad; it unties knots in your shoulders from a stressful day. Oh and the smells! I love good smells! Like my coconut and orchid shampoo.

After fifteen minutes in the shower, I know it's time to head towards Parkers. I dressed in my normal attire of hiking boots, jeans, and a nerdy long sleeve shirt. Not too snug. But with a set of 34DD boobs like mine everything is always a little snug. As I do a once-over in the mirror I see a more put together me.

My long hair is hanging down to the middle of my back in nice, long curls. After putting on a little makeup, my green eyes pop like it's Saint Patty's Day. My favorite necklace that hangs just above my breasts with its Eye of Horus charm bright and shiny. My dad gave it to me when

I was thirteen. It's supposed to give me good health and protection. Thanks to all the self-defense and kick boxing classes I teach, my body was toned but yet I still had ginormous boobs, and feminine curves. Thank god! Okay! I was feeling as good as I think I would be this week. Now it's time to head over to the bar.

Parkers is a sports bar owned by Ray Parker and his daughter, Candace. It was a 2400 square foot building set right in the middle of Norfolk. Great location. It happened to be in the middle between army, naval, and air force bases. While parking, I noticed Candace had finally talked her dad into updating the sign out front. She could be such a mouthy little devil to get what she wanted. Ever since that one fateful day in self-defense where she punched me (the assailant) in the gut and screamed "You're not getting a piece of my snatch, bitch!" She somehow convinced me we needed to be best friends after that.

Maybe it was the carrot cake she made me; I loved carrot cake more than any other food in the world! I took a look around as I opened the door, and no new surprise there, it is super slammed. People are hanging out at tables eating wings and French fries. People were lining up at the bar, and watching the games. But something hanging from the ceiling caught my eye. Red hearts? Cupid? Oh shit, Valentine's Day! I forgot Valentine's Day was this month. Could it really be February already? Maybe I could just tell the guys I owed them one.

Ever year around Valentine's, Candace tries to set me up with some hot guy in uniform, some sweet, muscular man that promises to make my Valentine's one to remember. So far none have prevailed.

There was Todd, sweet Todd from Kentucky that joined the army after high school. Not very bright, but very sweet. He had good old fashion southern manners. I decided I would give it a shot. I mean a gentleman always thinks of others before himself, right? Nope, he got the name three-minute Todd after that performance. Then there was body building Cade from the air force. One of those guys who you knew could just grab you by the butt, pick you up and impale you against the wall. Man I was excited about that one. Turns out he was a sensitive one. While we were getting hot and heavy he started crying because it was so beautiful, all the emotion. We spent the rest of the night watching Charlie St. Cloud. I loved that movie.

But before I could continue my thoughts on the last one, a high pitch scream demands my attention.

"Ah there's my little slut!" Candace Parker ladies and gentlemen!

"I hardly think I qualify as a slut, Ms. Candy wet T-shirt champion." She smirks.

"We all have to be good at something, Xena." Xena: Warrior Princess. She calls me that sometimes because of all the martial arts I do.

"I love the new sign, very bright." Her smirk turns into the cutest smile she's got. "I know!" she squeals.

"Finally he gave in. I told him what was the point of me going to college for a business degree if I couldn't put to use what I learned. That old sign was probably going to fall on someone and we would get sued." I took a look around. I saw my guys sitting at a table near the bar.

We made our way to the table. Once we arrived we got a loud cheer for a welcoming. I guess a few of them had already gotten the party started.

"Candy my love, will you get my boys here a round on me please?" The boys all hooted and yelled. I look at them.

"Thank you, guys, for helping out today at class, it wouldn't be the same without you. Truly from the bottom of my heart, thank you!" More cheers erupted from their mouths. Candace came back with the drinks. I grabbed a shot and downed the burning liquid quick. I grabbed another and held it up for a toast. Everyone followed my lead. I held my drink high and yelled "To upward thrusts!" Everyone yelled the same, and downed their drinks.

CHAPTER 2

DARIEN

Nine weeks. What the hell was I going to do for nine weeks? I was fine; the damn navy believed I was depressed. I was going to be depressed if I had to live a civilian's life for nine weeks! Christ! Being a Navy Seal was my life. The life of being a sailor, a leader. We kicked ass, and, well, we kicked some more ass. I took a swig of my beer from the bar. Parkers, the local sports bar.

Sitting next to me at said bar was my best friend since elementary school when we had a fight about your momma jokes, Captain Ross Olsen. He talked me into coming to this place to cheer up as he said and I quote "Get your vagina off the couch, time to nut up or shut up, dickweed." A charmer that one. He had been going on and on about a class where he got kicked in the nuts repeatedly today. He said the owner of Scars was going to be here and buy a round of shots for the guys who willingly got their asses handed to them. Who names a place Scars anyway, sounds like a douche, if you ask me.

"Dude, get your head out of your ass, you have a nine-week vacation. We should head up to the family cabin in West Virginia and go snowboarding," he says. I thought about it for a minute. "Let's do it!" I raised my bottle and clinked it with his.

My thoughts afterwards were put on hold when a female voice yelled "To upward thrusts!" Well, now that wasn't something you heard often. I had to turn to see who this ballsy chick was. I turned towards the noise and suddenly gasped for air.

Holy shit! Long, brown curls that reached her mid back. Creamy skin like French vanilla, a classic flavor you just want to taste over and over. Looking down and fuck! Those damn pants hug every curve of her like it was poured onto her. The type of body that was a sculptor's wet dream. Suddenly while staring at this goddess, a pair of shocking green eyes returned my stare. I think I forgot how to breathe. Something in those eyes held me.

Sadness? Curiosity? Desire? Then suddenly the goddess looked next to me and smiled. That smile could bring any man to his knees. The best smile I had ever seen in my life, then she started walking this way.

Wait. She was walking this way. *Breathe, fucker, breathe.* She stopped dead in front of us and spoke to Ross.

"Glad you made it! Thanks again for today." She hands him a shot which he happily takes and downs. What the fuck? How does the goddess know Ross?

"It was no problem, as I told you, I want to be a part of what you do." Okay what the hell was going on?

Ross turned to me and said, "Scarlet, I'd like you to meet my friend Darien Valentine." She turned those gorgeous green eyes on me and I saw something there. Amusement?

"Darien Valentine." My name coming off those lips automatically makes me want to go caveman on this goddess and take her back to my place and hear that name on her lips over and over.

Ross smacks my shoulder taking me out of my fantasy. "And this is Scarlet Barnette. She owns Scars, and teaches the self-defense class I am volunteering at." Well fuck me sideways. I shook out of my temporary paralysis and raised my hand.

"Pleased to meet you, Scarlet." She grabbed my hand and I felt a shock of ecstasy run through me and by the look in her eyes, she felt something too. She pulled her hand away, but before she let go my finger grazed her hand in a long stroke. The air felt thicker, more tense. She spoke "So, Darien, do you work with Ross at the station?" Trying to bring innocence back into the air, are we?

"Nope, just currently on a little R and R from the navy. "

"Navy huh? My friend Candace's brothers are in the navy. Oh Shit! Speaking of Candace, I will be right back!" She runs off, man she has got a really fine ass. A smack on the shoulder breaks me out of my staring.

"So, I think we found what you are going do to for your leave."

"That obvious?" I answered.

"Man she would eat you up and spit you out. Then kick your ass for fun." Hm I wouldn't mind that mouth on me.

"I got a lot of shit on my plate right now," I counter.

"I think you would be willing to make a little time out of your schedule out for her. But, dude, I'm going to be the big brother here. I like her, she seems nice. If you do make time for her, don't be a dick." Like that would happen. Funny hearing that from Mr. One-Night Stand himself.

Scarlet starts heading our way again, towing a short pixie behind her. "Hey, guys, I would like you to meet Candace Parker. She owns the bar." Candace was a short chick with black hair and brown eyes. She looked like a man-eater and by the way she is looking at the dumbass to my right it looks like she has chosen her next meal. I elbow Ross in the side.

"Hey, I'm Ross, this is my friend Darien. You've got a nice place here. Everyone has been very accommodating."

"Well we aim to please here at Parkers." Oh man, I think Mr. One-Night Stand has met his match. This was going to be fun to watch. I sneaked a peek at the goddess. She was looking at them like she could bust out laughing at any moment. She looked at her friend.

"Ross here volunteered at my class this morning. He's the captain Station 8 in Chesapeake."

"Oh that's so sweet of you to join Scarlet's cause to help women be able to kick some guys' asses, and also a firefighter." She licks her lips. "How courageous of you."

Oh shit! This was hilarious. I looked at Scarlet. It seemed she had a sense of humor trying to set them up. She looked at me and winked. I think I died and went to heaven. This girl was amazing.

Wait... What's happening to me? Candace's voice took me out of my self-observations. "Oh! We should go out tonight!"

"I'd love to, Candace. Darien, you in?" Ross asked me. I'm not sure I wanted to go with them just so I could watch them play tonsil hockey later.

"I think I'm good tonight, I got a lot of shit to do with the house tomorrow. You kids have fun though." Scarlet looks a little disappointed. Did she want me to go? Candace asked if she was going. She declined saying she had to get back to Roxy. Who's Roxy? Does she have a kid? I love kids but that would make it difficult for a little fun in the sun.

"Well I think I'm going to head out, I got my boys their drinks, and it has been a long day." She spoke then looked at me.

"It was nice meeting you." It was definitely nice meeting her.

"Pleasure meeting you as well." Something sparked in those emeralds.

Candace interrupted our little staring contest going on. "Okay, why don't we all go out tomorrow? We should go dancing! We love to dance!" I looked at Candace and the look she had was mischievous. What was that pixie up to?

"Oh hell yeah! That sounds like fun. You Debby Downers up for it tomorrow?" Ross belted out. I looked at Scarlet.

"Yeah, I'm down," I said. Scarlet agreed. Tomorrow was going to be an interesting night. Candace made plans with Ross for tonight, then they said their goodbyes and headed over to the table that they were at.

Ross sighed, "Man, I think I am in love." I laughed.

"Yeah, good luck with that one." I slapped him on the back.

"Alright, man. I'm going to get out of here; I've got a lot to sort through at the house." He just nods.

"Yeah, I hear you. If you need anything let me know." I started to head out, but I took a glance at Scarlet one last time before I left. She's laughing with the guys at the table. I wish I knew what made her smile like that. Suddenly she turned those emeralds on me and I was lost. She laughed and turned back to her table. I walked out into the night and headed home. My thoughts easily returned to Scarlet. Man I was in trouble.

CHAPTER 3

SCARLET

"Mammoth yeah, just like that!" "Oh Darien!" He kissed that spot behind my ear, and then nuzzled my neck with his scruffy chin. Oh my! I love scruffiness. He moved across my collarbone and back up to my jaw. He made a noise that sounded like a growl. Oh god, I was so turned on right now. His hand traveled down my stomach. Down. Down. OH MY! He went to whisper in my ear then he licks my neck. Interesting. He continued to lick my neck, and then my jaw, and my face. *WHAT THE HELL*? Realizing I was dreaming, I woke up. But why was I still being licked? ROXY!

"Down, Roxy!"

Such a good dream, now I had a slimy dog face. I turned over and thought about last night.

Darien Valentine, what a man! Black hair, that perfect hair-grabbing length. He had to be 6'2, broad shoulders, very muscular body. He had a body like an MMA fighter; and he gave off dangerous vibes like them too. He looked like the type of guy that left a line of broken hearts behind him, but boy did you love every minute of it. He had a sharp, scruffy jaw, and an imperial roman nose. And those eyes!

OH those eyes, the only way I could describe them was as "Beach eyes." Beautiful gold surrounding the pupils, just like sand at the beach, and then, suddenly, BAM! A deep blue like the ocean. I could stare into those eyes and never surface. Like an undertow, you would never see me again. Being close to him made me feel like my world was spinning.

I heard a whine from the side of the bed. "I'm sorry, girl. Let's go get you something to eat." Rolling out of bed, I walked down the stairs and got Roxy some food. I made a cup of stress tamer tea and headed towards my porch. I loved waking up to see the sunrise over the ocean. It's so peaceful here. The waves are calm over the sand; it's very quiet this morning. The sky was lit up with different shades of reds, oranges, purples, and a bit of blues.

Roxy came bursting out the door and down the porch stairs towards the beach. She loved playing in the water. I bet she missed Aunt Tara. She was such a carefree woman. Her whole life saying was Hakuna Matata. Yeah I know, but when you think about it, it is a nice way of living, always saying no worries to everything. I've tried to adopt the philosophy as well. Trying to live for today and enjoy life. I missed her already. I think I'll go over there and check on things.

I walked back into the house and set my tea cup down on the counter. I looked around my house. I always liked color. I've got terra cotta color see-through curtains hanging around my windows. Turquoise blue curtains hanging by my sliding glass door that leads out to the beach. I will leave that open, get some fresh air in the house. I walked over to open the door and stubbed my toe on my brown sectional. "OUCH!" Man, my day was just going great. First with my sexy dream turning out to be with a dog, and now I stubbed my baby toe. Great!

I grabbed my keys and set out to Aunt Tara's house. It looked so quiet and daunting. I walked up the porch and used my key to open the door. The smell of vanilla and lime assaulted my nostrils. She always loved tropical-like smells. Always buying candles, sprays, anything that smelt like a tropical drink. It looked the same as when she lived in this house. Her bright yellow couch was still sitting by the window with its flowery pillows and sky diving magazines littering the coffee table. Her china perfectly organized in the kitchen cabinets.

I made my way up towards her attic. I pass pictures of her family along on the way up the stairs. She really loved her family, especially her nephew; I forget his name. But she said he was a Navy Seal, so she didn't have many pictures of him. I noticed her bedroom door was closed. I wasn't ready to go there yet. A place where it was so her, with her crumpled up bedspread, because she never made her bed. A Percy Jackson book with dog-eared pages on the night stand. We were reading the series together. I pulled down her attic stairs and climbed up. There were many boxes to go through; I started with her books, then maybe I'll move on to her pictures.

After organizing her books, and going through three albums of her adventures, I heard a noise. A creak in the floorboards below. Was someone in the house? Oh god! Was there a robber here?

I ran over to the wall by the stairs leading up here. I would get this person! Being a self-defense teacher and a kick boxer came in handy in situations like this.

I listened as the noise creeps closer to the stairs. Okay, okay I was ready! The robber was walking up the stairs, and then came to a stop, and now a big body was standing in front of me looking around.

The body walked forward a bit. I tried to make my escape back down, but the person grabbed my shoulder and yelled "HEY!"

I slammed my elbow into the robber's gut, stepped on their instep of the foot! The person wrapped their arms around me and spun me away from the escape of the stairs. I broke free of their grasp on my arms and I grabbed their wrist and adjusted my knees to throw the robber over my shoulder. I started to run for the stairs when a hand grabbed my ankle, thus tripping me. I fell to the ground and the robber started pulling me towards them. I kicked my feet towards their face and the robber dodged my kicks. I spun around trying to get a look at the robber, when he attacked me. I knew it has to be a he based on the size and weight of the person. Plus, I would have been free by now if it was a female. He lunged at me knocking me on my back and pinned me down. I went for my next move to head-butt him and I stopped. I was being stared down by the only pair of eyes who could disable me. Beach Eyes!

"Darien?" I asked. He looked stunned, and now confused.

"Scarlet? What the hell are you doing in my house?" he demanded.

"I was organizing. Wait. Your house? I will have you know this house belongs to a dear friend of mine, Aunt Tara." He had a face that could say only one thing. DUH!

"Yeah, my aunt Tara left it to me after she passed. I just moved in yesterday." Nephew? Navy?

"HOLY SHIT! You're her nephew? The Navy Seal?" He looked a little smug. He glanced down my body and that's when I realized I was still in my tight Harry Potter night shirt that stopped right above my navel, and my plaid men's lounge pants, with no shoes and no bra! AH, how embarrassing! He made his way back up to my eyes. His eyes showed a hunger. I tried to move but he was still pinning me to the ground. "Can you let me go now?"

"Depends, are you going to attack me again?" he asked with a smile. My eyes narrowed.

"You attacked me! I thought you were a robber and you grabbed my shoulder!" He quietly shh'd me.

"It's okay, this is just an easy misunderstanding." He let go of my wrists and got up to sit down next to me. I sat up slowly and looked him over. His black hair was messy, his shirt and sweatpants were rumpled. I must have woken him up.

"Sorry if I woke you, I didn't think there was anyone in the house. I didn't know what was going to happen to it. But at least you aren't some pervy man that hangs out naked on the beach listening to salsa music, right?" He laughed a real hearty laugh. "Not today, no." Well at least something has gone right today; I was really worried about that one.

"Sorry I frightened you, would you like a cup of coffee?" he asked.

"No thank you, I don't drink coffee, but I will take some of Aunt Tara's tea. I know where it is." He stood and helped me up. He pulled me up a little hard and I slammed into him. His touch sent a shock to my core. I shivered. My hands were on his chest. He felt so hard, so muscular. I looked up and he was looking down at me. We were both caught in each other's stare. He coughed, then broke the connection. "Sorry, I'll go get some hot water going for you." He let go and headed down the stairs.

I let a breath out I didn't even know I had held in. After catching my breath, I thought about what Aunt Tara said about her beloved nephew. She used to tell me stories about him: how smart, funny, handsome and good at everything he was. She said he was a jack of all trades. He could build anything, and fix anything, and yet be gentle. He was a Navy Seal; I mean, he did say he was in the navy, but nothing about being a Navy Seal. I mean, those guys were the best of the best of the best, sir! Oh no, the movie quotes are coming out. I just quoted Men in Black in my head! The scene where Will Smith is taking a test with the other men and, STOP IT, SCAR! You need to be focused! Now get your butt down there and face him!

I headed down the stairs to see him reaching above his head to the top shelf to grab the tea cups. While he wasn't quite aware I was there I took a moment to really take him in.

Long muscled arms reaching high, pulling his shirt up enough that I got a glimpse of a really tight set of abs and V. Oh the V, one of my favorite parts of a man. You know the part where his abs and hip bones create a V that head straight down to my other favorite part of a man. Yum. He must have felt my presence because he looked over and smirked. SHIT! He caught me checking him out.

I walked over to the cabinets in front of him and grabbed the jasmine, orange tea. He was right behind me; I swear I heard him smell me. I could be wrong though. I turned around and he was making sure the water was heating up. I guess it was my imagination. We didn't say a word to each other until we were both settled at the kitchen table. The smell of jasmine and orange calmed me, as the coffee seems to be doing the same for him. It was getting kind of quiet then so I started conversation.

"I'm sorry about your aunt. She was one of my best friends. A very amazing woman." He looked a little sad.

"Yeah, she was great. It's weird being in this house surrounded by her, you know?" I looked around and I knew exactly what he meant. It's like she is just out on vacation and she would be back next week.

"Yeah, it's weird, I feel like she will be coming home from her routine sky diving trip any day now. But I know it's not true." He looked around, he had a questioning look on his face. "I thought she had a dog. Do you know what happened to it?"

"Roxy? Yeah, Aunt Tara left her to me. She's over at my house. I live in the house right next door." That seemed to answer some questions, even some maybe he didn't ask.

"That was very nice of you to take care of her. I haven't seen her since she was a puppy. I bet she's huge now!" I laughed thinking about how huge that dog was, and then I flushed thinking about the dream she interrupted me from this morning.

"Yeah, she is pretty big. Eighty-five pounds now," I said shyly.

"Nice, I love big dogs. German shepherds especially, they are so smart and can do anything; that's why they're used in the police force and military." Bringing up military made me think of his career.

"So, you're a Navy Seal. You must be very proud of yourself to get that honor. I bet you have travelled all over the world." He looked off, not really looking at anything in particular. "It has its benefits. And you own your own studio?"

"Yes, I opened Scars to help people gain confidence in themselves. By learning self-defense, you hold your head high because you know you can handle yourself. I do kickboxing as well. It's a great workout and works with the self-defense." He seemed amused a bit.

"Your moves are very good. I know I am a Navy Seal, but you really could hold your own against most everyone. Not sure you could beat me though." He winked! A challenge, huh?

"You should volunteer for one of my classes. We will see if I could take you." His right eyebrow lifted in challenge.

"I just might do that."

I heard a bark outside the door. Roxy must have been done chasing little crabs and was now wondering where I was. "Well, that is my alarm. Roxy is wondering where I am."

I stood up and started to head for the door. I heard him following behind me. "I would like to see this beast of a dog." I opened the door and Roxy bypassed me and went straight to barking at Darien.

"Holy dog, Batman!" he shouted. "Hey, that's my line!" I blurted out. He laughed. Oops I didn't mean to say that out loud.

"Roxy, sit." He spoke with authority in his voice. It even made me want to sit. Roxy sat, and looked up at him waiting for her next orders. He bent down and rubbed her head and patted her back. It was nice to see him so gentle. He looked like such a dangerous man. Dangerous and gentle, just thinking about those things put together in one man, made my insides quiver. I bet he was very adventurous and took control in bed but also the type of man that would make sure you always got your pleasure out of it before him. I shivered.

"Are you cold?" he asked, although with the hunger in his eyes I think he had an inkling about what I was thinking. My lips parted, I was stuck staring at him. He stood and came closer. He reached out and tucked a curl that was hanging in my face behind my ear. I gasped.

I was already falling under this man's spell. He came closer. Oh god, was he going to kiss me? What would I do? Would I kiss him back? Push him away? I just stood there waiting to see what was going to happen. He stopped just about an inch from my mouth. I could feel his breath on me. It shot a lightning bolt of pleasure down between my legs. My body felt warm, feverish. He whispered "Scarlet, what are we getting into?" I gasped. I needed to get out of there! I looked into his eyes and panicked.

"Bye, Darien." With that said I turned and walked back to my house, Roxy followed me. I swear I heard her sigh, like she was saying *geez, Scarlet, you almost had him.*

CHAPTER 4

DARIEN

I watched as Scarlet ran away to her house. What
just happened here? One minute I was petting Roxy then
the next I was about to go all caveman on that woman. I
would have kissed her, picked her up and carried her to
the couch. Oh god, the way my name sounded on her lips,
it was just like before at the bar! I just want to hear her say
my name over and over while I wrapped her legs around
me. Ah great! I needed to go take a cold shower. I made
my way upstairs and used the second bathroom. It was
still a little weird being in Aunt Tara's house, it still smells
like her. Well, thinking about my dead aunt was definitely
a way to get rid of my hard-on. I still took a cold shower
more or less as preventative care. I stepped out of the
shower and dried myself. I walked over to the window
thinking. I still can't believe the goddess I met last night,

the very same one that took up the main role in my dream last night, lived next door.

I look over towards the house and groaned. "Fuck!"

She was doing yoga on the beach. You'd think it was a little cold for it in February, but there she is, bending over, and then going into plank position, then she slowly lowers herself to the ground then arches her back up. I groaned again. She was wearing a sports bra that seems to be having difficulties holding in those DDs. That scrap of material she wore as shorts did nothing to hide her spectacular ass. She was toned in all the right places, but still had those soft feminine curves. Damn, I've turned into a fourteen-year-old again, where all you have to do is look at a chick and you get a hard-on. I am a Navy Seal for Christ's sake! Control yourself, man!

With a deep breath I walked away from my very own wet dream outside the window. I grabbed a pair of gym shorts and a shirt planning on cleaning up the house and moving things around. I couldn't stay here if it looked like Aunt Tara was going to walk in the house at any minute. Starting with the bedroom, I brought out some new sheets and a comforter I bought yesterday. I folded her quilt comforter and put it in the hall closet. As I organized and changed things up in the house I tried not to let my thought go towards my sexy new neighbor. Five hours of cleaning and making the house more habitable for me, and I still couldn't get Scarlet out of my head. I needed to get out of my head for a little bit, so I decided to go for a run. There was nothing like pounding the pavement and sweating all your thoughts out.

An hour and six miles later, I got close to the house when I heard music blaring from Scarlet's house. Sounds like... I've got to see this.

I quietly snuck up to her house and peeked in the window. I started laughing so hard I had to grab the railing to stop myself from falling over. Scarlet was inside cleaning. Not just cleaning like normal people. She was listening to "This Is How We Do It" by Montel Jordan, and was dancing/singing around while cleaning.

"Ever since I was a lower class G, but now I'm a Big G. Hundred dollar bills y'all," she sang. I haven't heard that song in forever. "Whatever it is, the party is underway. So tip up your cup and throw your hands up and let me hear the party say. I'm kinda buzzed and it's all because, THIS IS HOW WE DO IT!" she continued to sing out.

The more I watched her, the more fascinated I became. She seemed like such a free spirit, someone you could have both fun and serious conversations with. Someone who would keep you entertained. Some men had issues when it came to being with women, but not me. My parents were still happily married. I had been with a lot of women and enjoyed their company. I just haven't met anyone who has made me want to dive into forever. I had such a pull towards Scarlet, I really wanted to get to know her. Her likes, dislikes, quirks, her favorites, and favorite songs of the '90s. Well, why not have a little fun with her now.

She was organizing the bookshelf next to her sectional. I knocked on the door. No answer. I knocked again. Still no answer. I banged loudly on the door and that got her attention. She screamed then turned towards the noise in full on ready-to-kick-ass mode. She was cute, and about the only female I felt we could spar all day with and she would continue to surprise me with her moves.

It took her a moment, then she realized it was me. She turned down her music and walked over and opened the door but not quite wide enough to allow me inside. "What's up?"

"Heard you were having a party over here, it sounded like fun." I winked at her. She blushed.

"I like music when I clean, it makes it more fun." I looked around

"Mind if I come in? Aunt Tara doesn't have cable or any movies past the 1950s at her house. I like peace and quiet but it's a little too quiet." She nodded; I guessed she knew the feeling.

"Sure, come on in. I was thinking about ordering a pizza and watching a movie, sound good?" This was the perfect opportunity to figure this woman out.

"Sounds awesome! Mind if I use your bathroom though?" She pointed down the hall. "Yeah, go ahead." I walked down the hall. Pictures of her and her family were strewn about the walls. I found the bathroom and cleaned up a bit.

After feeling refreshed I headed back out. I stopped to look at a few of her pictures. There was a bunch with her and I am guessing her parents. She looked almost identical to her mother, except her eyes, those are from her dad. They look happy. I walked back into the room, I found her in the kitchen as she grabbed the phone.

"I like Little Italy's pizza, is that okay?" she asked

"Yep," I said as I looked around her place. Very colorful. She had orange looking curtains hanging from her windows. Turquoise curtains hung from her sliding glass door that led out to her backyard. Her space was organized but comfy. Her brown sectional had multi colored pillows and a big-ass red blanket that looked comfy as hell.

I continued to gaze around her house while she ordered our food. After looking at her wall décor and getting a glance at her book collection, I came to the conclusion that she was a bit of a geek.

Maybe it was the light saber hanging on the wall, or maybe it was the Harry Potter memorabilia that gave her away. But I could be wrong. Now that I think about it, wasn't she wearing a Harry Potter shirt this morning? It was hard to get past the whole no bra thing, but straining my brain to remember every detail I remembered she was. I hadn't even been here for ten minutes and I already had a deeper insight into the life that is Scarlet. Got to say it's amusing and cute. She sauntered over; I liked the way her hips sway. Just saying...

"It will be here in about twenty minutes. So what type of movies do you like?" she asked. Being a Navy Seal I really didn't have much time for movies.

"I like pretty much everything, although if you put in a chick flick I might just puke." She laughed.

"I think I know just the movie. I haven't seen it yet and I'm guessing you don't get too much time for movies." Yep, she guessed right. Smart one that girl. She laughed as she made her way to her huge DVD collection.

"Damn, I think you have more movies than any of my guy friends, impressive." She blushed again. This was getting to be a fun game, making Scarlet blush.

"Yeah, I really love movies," she said shyly. She put the movie in and then crawled onto the couch. She sat on one end and me on the other. Ah, the Avengers, I've wanted to see this movie. I turned to her. "You are a goddess! Not many chicks are into this stuff."

"Yeah, I don't know if you looked around at all but I'm kind of a geek." I laughed a bit.

"Yeah, I saw the light saber." Out of nowhere Roxy comes over and sits right in between Scarlet and me, then stares right at me as if to say *I'm watching you, bud... Hurt my girl, I'll hurt you.*

"Hey, foxy Roxy, you must be done with your treat," Scarlet said as she scratched behind the dog's ears. She looked at me then looked away quickly. After a few minutes she gets up. "I'm gonna get something to drink, would you like anything?"

"Yeah, I'll take a water." She left and came back with two bottles of water. She just about made it to the couch when she tripped on a dog toy and was heading towards the ground. I reached out and grabbed her so she wouldn't hurt herself. I suddenly became very aware that I was holding her in my arms. She was so close I could smell that coconut shampoo she uses. Her eyes went wide and her gaze went to my lips then back up. My thoughts went wild. I barely knew this woman and she already was making her way somewhere no woman had been before. My heart. The need to take her grew; I searched her face for any objections. I looked her in the eyes and almost closed the gap between us. She gasped.

Then the doorbell rang. FUCKING HELL! She shivered and shook herself out, as if to wake up from a spell. "Pizza's here!" She steadied herself then went to the door.

CHAPTER 5

SCARLET

Oh my god, oh my god, oh my god!!! I ran away from Darien as fast as I could. I was caught up in him and almost kissed him, AGAIN! That was the second time today I almost let him get me. Not that it would be a bad thing, but I was trying to turn over a new leaf here. Every relationship I have had, has been ruled by the physical stuff. Candace hasn't been much help either with pushing guys at me left and right. I wanted to get to know the guy and become friends before we give into the physical stuff. I felt like it might not be as much heartache.

I opened the door, got our pizza,, and gave the delivery man an extra tip just for saving me from kissing

Darien. I walked back over and put our pizza on the coffee table when my cell phone rang. I reached over and answered it. I winced as a loud, screeching voice attacked my ear.

"SCARLET!!!!!!!!!! Oh my god, girl, I am in heaven right now! I think I am in love, oh my god! Ross and I haven't left the condo since last night. He is amazing! AHHHH!" I had to pull the phone away from my ear at that last scream. Darien was looking at me curiously; I wonder if he could hear what she was saying. "With that being said, we are going to have to reschedule our dancing night tonight. I am not even close to being done with this man." I heard a man's voice in the background.

"Hell no you aren't, now get your sweet ass back in this bed!" I giggled. "Ok, Scar, I've got to go! I'll talk to you whenever we make it out of the condo." Then she hung up. Darien looked at me. "Guess we aren't going dancing tonight, huh?"

"Nope, seems like they are going to be holed up for a while." He laughed

"I warned him she would eat him alive." I laughed along with him. "Yeah she definitely is a man-eater, but maybe he will prove to be her match."

We both grabbed our slice of pizza and settled back into the couch. We were both very content in our silence and watched the movie. I kept peeking over at the gorgeous man on my couch. He seemed so relaxed. I was having fun laughing with him. He was very easy to be around. I wanted to learn more about him.

"So how do you know Ross?" He smirked a bit. "We both grew up around here. We went to school together, rode the same bus. The first time we met, we were in a your mamma joke battle. He said my momma was so fat that when she talks to herself it was a long distance call. Asshole. We got in a fight and somehow became best friends after that." I laughed. That was hilarious.

"That was a good one! Candace and I took self-defense classes with each other; she yelled at me about not getting a piece of her snatch then punched me in the stomach. Then she baked me a carrot cake and we have been friends for a few years now." We were both laughing now.

"So are you from around here?" he asked. "Nope, I'm from Asheville, North Carolina." He seemed to be committing that information to memory.

"Nice, the mountains, what brought you here?" I bit my lip and thought about how to answer without going into a whole different topic. "I was in a bad relationship and decided I needed a change of scenery. I've always wanted to live by the beach, and here I am." He looked like he wanted to press the issue but decided against it.

"Do your parents still live in Asheville?" he asked. "No, my dad is an archaeologist, and my mom is a writer. They are currently living in Cairo, Egypt." His eyebrows raised, he looked a bit impressed. Most people were when they found out what they do, and growing up getting to visit all kinds of places was pretty cool.

"Nice. My dad is a policeman and my mom is a dentist." He gave me a very cheesy smile. "See, perfect teeth!" I laughed.

"Very nice, glad to know that even Seals brush their teeth and floss." I winked at him. He laughed.

"Hey, just because we do dangerous missions, and sometimes are stuck out in interesting conditions doesn't mean you can forget your teeth. My mom would kill me!" He looked around like she might jump out at him. "I didn't know Seals were scared of anything," I teased. "Well, you haven't met my mother, she can be a peach."

Talking about our parents made me miss mine. I haven't spoken to them in a few days, but being so far away sometimes the reception was pretty spotty, especially when they were on digs. "What type of books does your mom write?" I looked at him, curious of what his reaction would be.

"She writes contemporary romance novels." He smirked. "Romance novels, huh? Nice." I decided to have a little fun with him.

"Yeah, you know the type of books where guy meets girl, they want each other so badly but don't give in, then something happens and they give into their primal needs, they fuck everywhere, lots of blow jobs, fall in love, go through something then have a happily ever after." His eyes turned a deep dark blue. He cleared his throat.

"Sounds like you've read quite a bit of those books." His voice was a little rough. "Oh yeah, hot guys, sex, love, happily ever after, I love them!"

Our gazes locked. He moved closer to me, I couldn't look away. I mean, I should. I should stop playing with him, but I kind of wanted to see what he would do. Maybe one kiss wouldn't be so bad. I've been kissed lots of times before. He stopped right next to me, our bodies angled towards each other like magnets. His voice was rough, and low. "Hot guys and lots of sex does it for you, huh?" He looked at my lips; I felt tingles all over my body.

"Oh yeah. You know, being slammed against the wall and---" Before I even finished what I was saying his lips were on mine. Our mouths moving over each other. He slowly licked my bottom lip, asking permission to let him in. I caved. I parted my lips and our tongues meshed together in an erotic dance and started caressing each other. He groaned at my acceptance then deepened the kiss.

I don't know how we got there but I was suddenly on my back and he was above me. This kiss was that good! Hands roaming everywhere they could as we continued to devour each other. I gasped a moan as we came up for air. His mouth never left me. He moved his lips over my jaw, then the part of my neck behind my ear and continued his wonderful assault down my neck. I moaned. There was a sound from the back of his throat, a half growl, half moan and then his movements got a little more possessive.

His hands ravished the curves of my waist. My hands slid up his back to the back of his neck, fingers snaked through his hair. His body was so warm. Pleasure and panic came over me. This was like no kiss I have ever had. This kiss would be my undoing. Shivers went all down my body and tension was building between my legs. On its own accord, my back arched and my hips came into contact with his, causing sweet friction. "OH God" I whispered. He pushed his hips down, and now I knew this man was a danger to me, with kisses like this, and, oh god, his hands. He also had an outstanding piece of man that was pressing against me. This was too much. My senses were in overload! I felt everything everywhere. If I didn't have him soon it felt like I would explode! That thought brought me back to reality. I had to stop this. I had never been friends with my lovers first, and it was always a dead end.

No more, Scarlet! Maybe this could be different. I stilled and stopped the kiss; he looked at me with a confused expression. "Are you ok?" he asked. His voice was laced with desire. It made it very hard for me to stop. My body was still craving him.

"I can't do this, I'm sorry." He started to rise off me and moved back. I got my body back in control and sat up; I looked at him hoping he wasn't mad at me. He didn't look mad. Thank god! He looked more concerned than anything. "I'm sorry, I feel like I have some things I need to explain." He shh'd me. "No, you don't. You don't owe me anything." Aw gosh he was too sweet. "No, it's ok, you are amazing and I need to let you know what's going on with me before this goes any further."

I took a deep breath. He put his hand on mine, and for some odd reason I truly felt comforted. Weird. I looked into those beautiful beach eyes as I spoke.

"Right before I turned eighteen my parents were in Nevada working on a site that supposedly had skeletons older than what we had seen before. On their ride back to the hotel they were hit by an older woman who was so close to being blind. They were in a coma for about eight months. During those eight months I worked and took care of our house. I met a guy named Frank; he was hot, sweet, and from New York. I was hooked. We got physical right away and never really got to know each other. He soon got very possessive of me, the jealous type, you know? He would freak out when I wanted to go anywhere where men would be present. I wasn't as confident then, and he was there through everything with my parents so I really depended on him and the attention he gave me."

Getting towards the hard part, I looked towards my shaking hands and I started to tear up a bit. I was no longer that shy, broken girl. I could do this. "The man that I ended up falling in love with was not the man I got. I was hanging out with my best friend, Shelly, at this lounge in downtown Asheville. Some guy came over and was talking to Shelly and me, we were having a very harmless conversation, when Frank came in and beat the guy to about an inch away from dying. Then he dragged me out of the lounge and beat me. He left me there after the sirens started getting close.

"The cops pressed charges and filed a restraining order on him. I thought everything was going to be good after that. But while I was at work he surprised me and he came at me with a knife." I shuddered.

I still remembered what he said to me. *You stupid bitch, I love you. You are going to be with me or no one else!* A hand came under my chin and lifted my head until our gazes met. His eyes were filled with empathy and concern. I felt things I didn't want to feel. I quickly shoved back those not so foreign feelings.

"I remembered some moves from one of the self-defense classes my mom and I took as research for one of her books. I broke his nose and some of the guys from the kitchen grabbed him and held him until the police came.

Sadly, he still got me on my right shoulder; it wasn't real deep but enough that I needed stitches."

Darien looked at my shoulder, and raised his hand to touch it. He looked up at me as if asking a silent question to see it. I nodded. He slowly moved my sleeve up till the three-inch scar was showing. "Fuck, Scarlet!" His thumb grazed over it very softly. I shivered.

I had never let anyone touch my scar besides medical personnel. He leaned forward and kissed it. My head fell back as his lips grazed my shoulder. It's like he was taking away all the bad memories and replacing them with his kisses. He coughed to clear his throat then sat back up. I could see he wanted to continue with his mouth on me but knew now was not the time.

"So what happened?" he asked. "He went to prison for attempted murder. I decided to move away, and I owe my life to those self-defense moves. So I decided to take as many classes as I could, then decided I wanted to give the knowledge that I had learned to other women so that they would be able to defend themselves like I had. That's why I named my place Scars, because of my name but also because of the scar, and scars that have been left behind. People don't need the scars I have. I can help them." He took my face in his hands.

"You are amazing, Scarlet. You are so brave and confident."

He softly kissed my forehead, then I was in his embrace. His strong, muscular arms surrounded me making me feel safe. "So after that I was with some men and it was all physical, but then I decided after all that I was going to be friends first with the next guy." I felt him smile. He gave me a little squeeze.

"After all the talk of hot guys and sex, what you really want is friends first huh?" I laughed. He spoke again, "Well, friend. It is getting late, how about we call it a night. I'll see you tomorrow, okay?"

"Sure, friend. I'll see you tomorrow." I smiled as I spoke. This was sweet. He gave me once last squeeze then let go and got up to leave. After he left, I got up then tripped over Roxy. Geez what a day. "I'm sorry, baby, I didn't see you there." I totally forgot she was around.

Getting up off the floor, I headed back upstairs. I was definitely in need of a shower. Maybe a cold one?

CHAPTER 6

DARIEN

After leaving Scarlet's house I walked up the porch and into my house. I needed a drink; I walked over to the fridge and grabbed a beer. Taking a big swig of my drink, I felt the cold liquid taming the fire inside my body. I still remembered the way her lips felt against mine, the way she tasted. I had never felt anything like that. I've made a few rounds when it comes to women but nothing has ever felt so good, so right. Her body just melting in my hands. I wanted to spend days just mapping out every inch of her body. And now I needed a cold shower. I headed upstairs and turned on the water. As I step in and let the cold water run over my back I feel a little at ease. My body still craved more of her but at least I can hold off a bit longer, otherwise I would have to take things into my own hands, if you get my drift.

Damn, I still can't believe her story about that dick she used to date. The thought pissed me off to no end that someone tried to hurt her. I wanted to hunt that fucker down and kick his ass. I've met guys like that; they play the sweet guy then flip their shit and turn into crazy, insecure assholes. At least that prick was in jail now and can't get her. God, I've only known this woman for twenty-four hours and already I feel the need to be there for her in any way. She says she wanted to be friends with her lovers first. Well dammit, I'm going be the best damn friend she has ever had. The cold water did its job. I stepped out of the shower, dried off, and grabbed a pair of sweats. I turned the TV on and fell on the couch. I slowly drifted into a dream about me, Scarlet, and a Princess Leia slave costume.

Damn, I fell asleep on the couch. I stretched my neck and shoulders, everything felt stiff. I needed coffee. I wondered what time it was. I think I got back from Scarlet's around 11:00. "Shit, eight thirty!" I had a meeting with the Lieutenant Commander at 9:00. I started the coffee pot and ran upstairs to get dressed.

Dressing in my navy shirt, uniform pants, and boots I ran back down the stairs. I stared at the coffee maker practically jumping with impatience. "Come on, coffee!" I grabbed my thermos and put my cream in. I heard a BING, thank god! I grabbed the pot and poured the coffee in the cup. After making sure the lid was secure I grabbed my keys and ran out the house towards Aunt Tara's Jeep. As soon as I was inside I turned the heat up. February in Virginia could be brutal sometimes. I switched gears and peeled out of the driveway. I only had twenty minutes to get across town to Little Creek.

I pulled into the base at 8:55. I cut the engine, opened the door and ran out towards the office. I made it to Lieutenant Commander Austin's door, I knocked and walked in. I looked over to the desk and saw L.C. Austin. I stood at attention and saluted.

"Alright, Valentine let's get to business." I lowered my hand. He gestured for me to sit. Besides initial hellos we were pretty laid back with each other. I sat.

"Listen, Valentine, with your team member Summers's death and the death of your aunt I know you have been through a lot. I wanted to talk over options of what you would like to do after your leave is up. We would be thrilled to keep you on your team. You are a superior sailor. We can put in for any orders you choose. But I also wanted to put out there that we could also use your superior skills to train the next line of Seals. You were the top of all your classes, especially combat and survival training. You would stay in Norfolk and work on base." That was definitely a bomb to my thoughts. I guess I just assumed I would go back to my team. Was I done?

"Thank you, sir. I'll have to think on that. I would like to get back to my team as of now, but I will take your offer into consideration." He walked over and gave me a good old fashion slap on the back.

"You're a good man, Valentine. But I worry about you; you have no life besides the military. You need something to keep you grounded. Enjoy your leave, go skiing, or find yourself a girl." He winked at me. I laughed

"Yes, sir!" He walked back around his desk and spoke. "Alright, get out of here." We shook hands and I left.

On my way to the car my cell phone rang. "Valentine," I answered.

"VALENTINE!! What's up, man?" I laughed. I guess Ross and Candace have taken a break from their marathon sex.

"Just leaving base, finally getting a breather, huh?" He laughed.

"Man, Candy is amazing! She does this thing with her tongue. AH god, now I'm hard. But no, man, I'm at work, otherwise I'd still be in bed with that woman. How are you holding up?" he asked. "Good, man, I met my neighbor yesterday."

"Is she hot?"

"Smoking hot, but get this. It's Scarlet." All I heard was coughing on the other end of the line. Ha! I bet he choked on that information.

"No shit? That is awesome," he muttered

"Yeah, man, she came into the house early morning yesterday to organize Aunt Tara's stuff. She woke me up. I thought there was a burglar in the house, but apparently she did too, as soon as I got up in to the attic we started sparring. She's got some really great moves. She kicks ass. We had pizza and watched The Avengers later on. Dude, she is amazing." Silence.

"You slept with her, didn't you?" I laughed. Oh I would have sold my soul to have that woman in bed with me last night.

"No, man, she wants to be friends first. She's just a cool chick, she loves comics, and action movies, and she dances to old '90s songs." Ross was laughing on the other line; I gave him a few minutes to get himself reigned in.

"It's only been a few days and we've both got it bad. Alright, man, I got to get back to work, but maybe sometime we can all go out and do something."

"Sounds good, later!"

I hung up the phone and stashed it back in my pocket. I turned the car on and headed to the store. An hour and a half later I pulled back into my driveway. As I came to a stop I looked over at Scarlet's house, nobody was home. I bet she had classes today. I grabbed the grocery bags out of the Jeep and carried them inside. I got done putting everything away, not sure what to do now. For about eight years, ever since I was eighteen, I had done nothing but what the navy assigned me to do. I looked out the back door and saw the beach. It's a little chilly today to be in swim trunks, but it's still be nice to hang out on the beach. I changed into a pair of jeans, grabbed a towel and headed out to the beach.

I closed my eyes and thought. I missed my team. We had all been together since A school. Ericson, the comedian, he always knew how to lighten the mood. Tanner, the bookworm, it took a while but we finally got him to learn street smarts and trash talking. The first time he ever trash talked he said, "You, sucker! Get out of my face before I beat you down." We were so proud, but obviously he needed a little more work. Daniels, he was always our chameleon. He could do anything, be anyone. Then Summers, he was just a fun kid, always happy, never let anything get him down. I was the leader, their captain, watching out for everyone. Making sure everyone had their shit in line. Great job I did.

Our last mission we were assigned to go and get a hostage on a boat out in the South Pacific. Easy enough. Water missions were our specialty. After a smooth snatch and grab we were on our way back to our boat when one of the terrorists who was hiding jumped out and shot Summers. We took the guy down, but it was too late. Summers was gone. You think you are trained and can deal with that shit, I mean everybody dies, right? But when it's someone you had been close with, you watch their back and they watch yours. It's never easy to deal with when one was gone. I hadn't been able to sleep for days since his death. Until Scarlet that is. Something about her, not just her body, but the way she made me feel. She was so brave, so strong. She made me want to be brave and strong as well. I sat and listened to the waves and slowly I drifted off.

"BOO!" I woke up in a panic and immediately went into Seal mode. I grabbed the person who scared me and pinned them down in the sand. Once my foggy brain cleared I noticed that I was once again pinning Scarlet down. She tried to put her hands up as if to surrender.

"Hey there, sailor, no harm!" she laughed. I guess I wasn't dangerous enough for her.

"I think I disagree with you there. Are you a spy? Sneaking up on me?" I leaned a little closer to her. Her face went very serious. Oh shit, now I've scared her. She looked around then leaned in closer. I was just about to tell her I was kidding when she said, "Oh no, my cover has been blown. What are you going to do with me?" She batted her eye lashes.

Fuck, she was playing with me. Lust swirled in my veins; my heart started racing at the fantasies that raced through me.

"I think I might have to take you in, check you for bombs or any other weapons." She shrieked, then she caught me in my momentary surprise, got out of my pin and took off running towards her house screaming, "You gotta catch me first, dirt bag!"

"Oh it is on!" I dug the ball of my foot into the sand and took off after her. Didn't take too long, I reached out to grab her, she juked me then tripped down to the floor.

"Damn door lip!"she muttered. I laughed so hard I fell to the ground. She pouted and smacked me on the shoulder. "You would make a terrible spy," I said in the middle of laughing.

"Yeah well, I would have made a kick-ass escape if the door lip didn't jump out and surprise me," she huffed out.

"You know I'm starting to see that you are a bit clumsy. I could be wrong though." Her chin came up in defiance.

"I'm not clumsy. The world of inanimate objects is just out to get me." I laughed. God this woman was a riot. I hadn't laughed this much is ages.

She was still pouting that I was laughing at her. "Any who, I saw you out there and wanted to see if you wanted to hang out." I wondered how long I was asleep out there. "What time is it?" I asked.

"It's about three thirty, you got somewhere you have to be, sailor?" Wow, I guess all those nights of no sleep were catching up to me. She smiled at me; it made me smile just knowing I was the one putting that smile on her face.

"Nope, no plans for me. What did you have in mind?" She looked back at the house. "I was about to take Roxy for a walk around the neighborhood, if you wanted to join." A walk did sound good.

"Sounds like a plan. Afterwards you guys can come over and I'll treat you to my famous quesadillas. You won't regret it, I promise." Her right eyebrow raised in suspicion.

"Your famous quesadillas, huh? I guess I can't turn that honor down." I looked her dead in the eyes. Trying to keep a serious face.

"Just getting to taste anything of mine is an honor." She smirked at me.

"Sounds like I will have to taste everything then."
She winked at me then got up to go get the dog. This bantering back and forth with her was going to make it hard for me to stick with that whole friends before lover's thing. I just wanted to kiss that smirk right off her face.

CHAPTER 7

SCARLET

I haven't had this much fun with a guy in so long. It was really refreshing. I just hope I can keep it in my pants longer. I truly enjoy it when a man manhandles you. Which is weird, I will admit, since I have gone through what I had gone through. Plus, I could kick a guy's ass now, so it's just like OH GOD YES when a guy pins you or picks you up and pushes you against the wall. Darien pinning me to the ground again almost did me in.

After seeing Darien sleeping on the beach I couldn't resist myself to sneak up on the guy. Stupid door lip! I could have gotten away too if I didn't trip. I walked over to the window seat where Roxy was manning her post. She liked it because she could look out the window and see what creatures came into the perimeter of the house. "Roxy, do you want to go for a walk?" She looked at me, ears at attention, and barked.

"Doesn't she need a leash?" Darien asked. Roxy tilted her head to the side like *what is a leash?* "No, she's completely trained to walk without one." We walked out of the house and down the stairs to the road.

Even though it's February now, the weather hasn't been too drastic. But I can tell we are probably going to get some colder weather soon. "How were your classes today?" Darien spoke.

"Great. I have one class that is going to be graduating soon. I always feel so proud when I have a class graduate. I feel good knowing I have helped them. Did you have a nice day?" He was staring off, nowhere particular. I wonder what he is really thinking.

"Yeah, just had to go down to base and talk with my Lieutenant Commander about some options for me after my leave." I let that soak in.

"Options? Don't you just go back to being a Navy Seal going on dangerous missions and such?" He laughed.

"I can, I've also been offered to stay here and train a new groups of Seals. I'm only twenty-six so it's not like I am burnt out, but maybe it would be nice to settle down a bit." I could see him settling down. Getting married and having a bunch of kids. The pain in the pit of my stomach I got from thinking about the lucky lady who he would choose was unsettling. I couldn't get jealous. He wasn't even mine for Christ's sake!

We fell into a comfortable silence, just listening to the breeze. Roxy was enjoying her walk as well. Panting and prancing along. We came to a park with a pier and decided to walk down the pier. I truly loved living by the beach. It was so serene. Seagulls were flying above; it was low tide so you could see little fish swimming around. I closed my eyes and just enjoyed the sounds of the scenery.

"Thanks for letting me join you and Roxy on your walk. It's very soothing being out in the open air," he said breaking through the silence.

"You're welcome. I couldn't agree with you more; it is very soothing. I just love it out here, any problems you have just seem to go away." We stayed on the pier for the sunset then headed back to the house. We made little chatter on the way back home about our favorites. So happens he and I have a lot in common. We both love '90s music. We had a lot of the same favorites among movies, besides my girly movies. Of course being a geek has its advantages too; we both like comics but disagree on our favorites. I love Rogue from X-Men, and he is a Wolverine fan. We both like Star Wars, but the biggest bomb he dropped on me, HE HADN'T SEEN ANY OF THE HARRY POTTERS! Ah, I could die right there. I mean, who hasn't seen at least one of them? Even if you don't like them, you still have seen one! I vowed to pop his HP cherry tonight if it's the last thing I do.

We got back to the house. He promised me his famous quesadillas earlier, but I needed to shower first. We split ways. As soon as I got inside, I got Roxy some food and headed for the shower.

After washing out the day's grime I dressed in my yoga pants and a nice V-neck T-shirt. Got to at least look a little good, right? My hair was still a little damp but I'd just air dry the rest. I grabbed a couple of movies, a chew toy for Roxy, and then headed over to the sexy neighbor's house.

As I opened the door my senses were assaulted by the most delicious aroma I have ever smelled. I followed my nose to the kitchen where Darien was cooking, wearing a gray T-shirt that hugged every one of his muscles on his broad shoulders, not leaving much to the imagination of just how cut he is. His jeans hung low on his hips, and at the bottom of those sexy jeans his bare feet were sticking out. Something about a man in the kitchen barefooted. Quite the change of roles I will say, but damn it's a sight, let me tell you. I guessed he sensed my stare. He looked over at me and smirked. "See something you like?" he teased. I turned my stare at those beautiful eyes.

"Looks so delicious." I walked over to him with a little more sway in my hips than I normally would. "Mom, oh god, I can't wait to try those quesadillas." He coughed a little then went back to cooking. I enjoyed teasing him like this; it was empowering to know I could affect him so much. I left the kitchen before he tried to get me back for teasing him. Roxy settled herself on the floor by the door leading out to the beach with her chew toy. She looked very content. I'm glad she didn't feel sad being back in this house.

"So I brought a couple of movies, figured we could hang out after dinner. Unless you have other plans?" I asked as I watched the dog. I didn't see him come over to me until I felt his breath behind my ear, causing shivers to go down my body. I was very aware of my surroundings.

"Oh, I have plans, but none that involve leaving the house tonight." I gasped. I couldn't control it. That just sounded so good. I mean we were getting along, right? Becoming friends? Warm sensations shot straight down to my core at the thought of spending the night with Darien. Tension building below. Christ, just his voice turned me on to this magnitude, I don't know if I would be able to handle it if he actually touched me again. My thoughts were brought back to that kiss on the couch. I bit my lip at the thought. Hands touched everywhere. Our mouths caressing each other. Oh he tasted so good. Our hips were moving together, the feel of his hard body against mine. *OKAY, ENOUGH!*

I turned to him, seeing the same passion in him as I felt. This was going to be a long night. "Are you plotting on me, Darien?" His eyes grew dark with the sounds of his name on my lips. I guess he liked hearing that.

"I wouldn't say plotting, more like positive planning." he said. I laughed "Troublemaker." He tucked a piece of damp hair back behind my ear. "You're so beautiful." I blushed "Thanks, you are too." He chuckled a bit.

"Beautiful, huh? Not quite like the guys you read in your romance novels." For some reason I just couldn't resist teasing him. I couldn't help it at all. "Well it depends, you've got the hot guy part so I guess it depends if you like to fuck a lot and fall in love." SHIT! Why did I say that last part? I mean I love those parts in the books. Where they do it all the time, but they fall in love and last forever. But I didn't want him thinking that's what I was looking for. Yikes. I had already screwed this up before it started. I didn't want to see his expression so I turned my back to him and started playing with my movies. He wouldn't let me cop out and gently turned me back to face him. He lifted my chin to look him in the eye.

"I could spend months fucking and pleasuring you." Oh god, what hearing him say that did to my body? My body heated, every nerve was a live wire just ready to explode with feeling. I was already very hot for him, but now it intensified from a soft fire to a freaking bonfire with gunpowder.

"As for the falling in love part. Who knows?" Well he wasn't running away. It didn't sound like he wanted to fall in love but wasn't opposed either. I'll take it; as long as he didn't run away from me I was good.

I tried to play it off like I didn't care either way. "Closet romantic are we? I just might be able to get you to watch The Notebook with me, huh?" He laughed.

"No matter how much I love a woman, I will never watch that movie." The mood got a lot lighter after that. He brought our food over to the couch while we settled in to watch a movie. I put in the first Harry Potter. He didn't seem to care or he seemed open to it at least. His food was delicious, definitely famous worthy. I kept moaning and complimenting him over how good it was; he kept shifting the way he was sitting a lot. It was weird. The couch wasn't as big as mine. Aunt Tara never really sat down much.

After the movie was over, he told me he liked it and to go ahead and put the next one in. I did so, then came back to the couch to find him sprawled out more. "I needed to stretch out a bit. But if you want, I have a very comfy nook here for you." He pointed to the nook right where his shoulder and chest met. Tempting. Why not? I shrugged and went to lie down in the nook.

"This is a mighty comfy nook, sir." He smiled and chuckled. "You're welcome to use it anytime." We both fell silent, just enjoying being with each other. It felt very natural. The way we had been around each other today had turned into a comfortable flirting. Not going too far but not totally innocent either. I was okay with that. We clearly wanted to tear each other's clothes off but neither one of us was pushing it, just kind of letting things progress as they were. I smiled at the thought and snuggled into his nook more and ended up drifting off to sleep.

CHAPTER 8

DARIEN

Sometime during the movie, Scarlet fell asleep in my nook. The movie was long done, but I just couldn't bring myself to wake her. I just lay there for a while looking at her. She looked so calm and comfortable. Her rosy pink lips were parted slightly; her nose was cute as it came to a little point. She had a very light dusting of freckles on her nose. I noticed a little scar laced in her left eyebrow. I wondered if it was from that dick she dated. I lightly ran my thumb over the scar. I wished I could take away all of the painful memories she had. She felt so warm in my arms, so natural, so right. I felt myself wanting to be like this all the time. That feeling brought me back to an earlier conversation with her.

She mentioned fucking a lot and falling in love were things she likes in books. Those things would both be so easy with her. Of course the first thing isn't a problem for me. I already had imagined all the ways I wanted Scarlet. As for falling in love? My dad always said he knew right away my mom was different. It took her a little longer to come to terms with being in love with him, but he always knew. I think I was falling in love with this brave, beautiful woman. She was clumsy, she made me laugh like no one else, and everything just felt the way it's supposed to. I know we hadn't known each other long, but it just felt right with her. Now I just have to show Scarlet that she was in love with me too. She moaned then rolled into me, her legs tangled with mine, her hand rested on my chest. Her upper body was pressed into mine. I felt a little daring and hugged her slightly and kissed her forehead. She stirred. Crap. I woke her. So much for being a stealthy Seal, huh, Valentine? Her eyes slowly opened and settled on my face. She didn't move away from me; that's a good sign. "Hi." Her voice was rough with sleep, but super sexy. "Hi." I smiled at her.

"Sorry I fell asleep on you. I guess I am just tired from my classes today." She still wasn't trying to get up. I liked this. "It's okay, why don't you go back to sleep, I don't mind." She looked at me searching for something. I guess she found what she was looking for. She nodded and closed her eyes. She snuggled even closer, which I wouldn't have thought possible. Her body fit with mine like it was made for me.

"You smell really good," she said quietly. I smiled and tried not to laugh out loud. I eventually fell asleep, thinking about the girl in my arms.

A noise woke me from my very nice dream. Scarlet and I were together playing spy on the beach, except unlike our real life version yesterday, she didn't trip. I caught her, and then I stripped her down looking for weapons. That same noise rang in my ears again. I slowly opened my eyes and took in the morning. I was immediately startled by a big dog head that was staring at me. Roxy must need something. I felt a little different than when I went to sleep. That's when I realized Scarlet was no longer in my nook but lying on top of me. I mean, I know the couch was a little snug for both of us lying on it, but I guess she preferred me as her pillow instead.

Don't get me wrong, I liked the way we were, but how to wake her up without her freaking out that she was lying on me with morning wood. What? It happens. Roxy was getting impatient with me that I wasn't getting up fast enough for her. She whined a little more. "Roxy, I'm coming, shhh." I spoke as quietly as I could. I swear the dog knew she had me in a position. If a dog could do the creepy evil grin, she would be doing it now. She barked. Scarlet's eyes flew open wide. She looked over at the dog.

"Good morning, baby, how did you sleep?" She clearly wasn't talking to me. She had to have noticed what she was sleeping on. Right?

Well no time like now to tell her. "Good morning to you too." Her hand started moving around my body. Not in a sexual way but a before-I-look-into-the-eyes-of-my-pillow-I-want-to-make-sure-it-really-did-talk, type of feel around. But I will say her feeling me up did push a little more blood down below causing my pants to get a little tighter. Which she obviously felt. "OH MY GOD! I AM SOOO SORRY!" She tried to get off me as fast as possible, but in the process she tripped and kicked me in the nuts as she went down to the floor.

"FUCK!" I yelled. I immediately grabbed my boys and tried not to vomit. My whole body was breaking out into sweats. I would take getting shot any day compared to the feeling of getting kicked in the nuts. I was too focused on the pain to hear her get up, but as soon as my eyes opened I saw she was talking to me.

"I don't know what's happened to me, I swear I am never this clumsy! Oh my god, are you okay? I am so sorry again! First I slept on you all night, then this." I shh'd her.

"SHH, it's okay, I just need a minute." She ran into the kitchen and got me some water. I took the cup and took a sip, it helped a little. I sat up. She was looking at me, obvious concern in her expression. Her hair had that just woken up shape to it. Her lips were a little pinker. Her skin had the barest blush to it. She was breathtaking. "You look beautiful in the morning." She blushed more. I couldn't stop staring at her.

"Thanks, I bet I have bad breath though. Do you want some coffee?" She said my magic words. Coffee.

"Yeah, I'd like that. Help yourself to some tea since I know you don't like coffee." She smiled at me. I will forever keep tea in my house for her. "Thanks. I'm going to go let Roxy out real quick."

She got up and let the dog out. Even though the morning had an interesting start to it, everything still felt natural. We flew into effortless conversation over coffee and tea, just like the other day. Just talking about everything. She really enjoyed photography, I told her about some stories with the Seals, then I told her about Summers. She reached over and placed her hand over mine. She was comforting me. It really seemed like it was helping, just knowing she was there for me.

"I'm sorry, that must be very hard for you." It was hard. "Summers was a kick-ass kid, I think he even had a girlfriend back home. I bet she is in a lot worse shape than I am in. I know he wouldn't want me to beat myself up over everything that happened. But as their leader I can't help but feel responsible for what happens to them. Even if it's out of my control." I looked out the window and thought about that day.

"It will be hard, but you will be okay. You are a strong man. You can move forward. You should embrace life and enjoy it. Try not to dwell on things you can't change." I looked at her. That sounded a lot like something Aunt Tara would say. The more I was around Scarlet, the more I saw a lot of Aunt Tara too. It was comforting.

"Yeah, you're right. So what are you up to today?" I asked, trying to move on from that subject.

"I have a few classes then I have some paperwork I have to work on at home for a while. Probably won't go out tonight, You?"

"I'm thinking about going and visiting my family today. I haven't seen them since I got in." I should have called to let them know I was in town, but I know my mom is having a really hard time with my aunt's death. I haven't wanted to be around more people who are sad and who will make me feel even more like shit about death. The only person who I haven't had to walk on egg shells around is Scarlet. Even though she has lost one of her best friends she keeps on going, not looking back. LIGHTBULB!!

"Do you have any classes tomorrow?" I blurted out. "Yes, I have two in the morning." Perfect!

"I know this is a little out there, but would you like to come with me to my parents' house tomorrow? Not as a date or anything. I think with everyone being sad about Aunt Tara's death, you might liven up the place a bit." Not to mention how much more comfortable I will feel with her there, but she didn't need to know that right now.

"Hm, I'm not sure. I wouldn't want to impose." Not a no...

"It would be no problem at all! Come on. Please?" I put on my best begging face. She caved.

"Oh alright, put those puppy eyes away. God, you shouldn't use those things on people. It's hardly fair." Puppy eyes? I guess my begging face is very convincing. To play or not to play?

"So what you're saying is that all I have to do is give you puppy eyes and you will do anything I want?" I gave her a very wolfish grin. Her eyes narrowed at me.

"Don't abuse your power, Mr. Valentine." I chuckled. "I wouldn't dream of it, Ms. Barnette."

"Well on that note, I better get a move on before you use your Jedi mind tricks to make me do something dirty." She scrunched her face up and stuck out her tongue at me. I wanted to bite it. She took her cup to the sink and then headed towards the door. "Wait, I know we live next to each other but I don't even have your number. You know, for tomorrow," I pointed out. "Oh yeah, right, my number." She walked over to the counter, grabbed a pen and paper, and wrote her number down.

"Alright, Darien, I will see you tomorrow. Let's go, Roxy!" The dog looked pretty comfy but she got up and ran out the door. "Bye, Scarlet," I said.

Chapter 9

Scarlet

Sigh, paperwork. After my classes today, I grabbed a drink, my laptop, put in Mamma Mia, and started on my paperwork for the business. Typing reports of last month's profits and losses. Thankfully I didn't have to spend much. Also those drinks for the guys are a tax write-off! I loved being a business owner. It's so freeing to decide your own schedule. You can take off time when you want, time like after class tomorrow. I still can't believe Darien invited me to go to his parents' house with him. I felt very comfortable around him, like we were friends, but I didn't want his parents to think we were together. I don't think Darien was the type of guy to do relationships. Even though I was getting to know his character, he still looked dangerous to a woman's heart. Especially since he was letting his scruff on his face grow, oh I loved facial hair. It really completed the edgy appearance he had going on. I really was starting to like him. His nook was so comfortable; I hoped I could sleep without it tonight.

I threw my head into the pillow and screamed. "AHHH." I can't believe this. I can't even say I was starting to like him. I really liked him. He listened to me. He was funny, we just meshed well together. If only we were like Sophie and Sky in Mamma Mia singing Lay All Your Love on Me. I felt like a sitting duck when it came to him. Maybe this was good though. I mean, he was pretty perfect. I guess we will see. Right now I need to focus on my work.

Around ten o'clock, I hear a knock at the door, and was secretly hoping it was Darien. That he was thinking about me today like I had been thinking about him. "Scarlet!!" Nope, it was my BFF, Candace. I could use a girl's night. "Hey, babe!" We hugged and went back inside.

"So how have you been? You have to catch me up on the gossip." Candace spoke as she poured us each a glass of wine. "What makes you think I have any gossip?" Trying to show the most secretive facial expression I could.

"Oh come on, Scar. A little birdie told me about the hot new neighbor, you have to have gossip!" I laughed.

"This little birdie doesn't happen to be your sex marathon partner does he?" She moaned.

"Oh god, yes! So dish." I told her about everything that has happened since we parted at the bar.

"Wow! Scar, that is so hot and you kissed him! How was it? He looks like he could just turn you into a puddle on the floor. Please tell me I am right." I thought about that kiss the other night. My body turned warm, I could still feel his hands all over me. I pressed my knees together trying to release some of the pressure building in my core.

"Mmm, I... it was amazing. He totally melted me, and then I ended it. Ugh why did I do that." She patted me on the back.

"Because of your whole friends before sex thing. I support you on whatever it is you want to do, but, man, you should be doing him! I don't know if this thing with Ross will turn out to be something, and right now I am just enjoying him and his penis. It's mutual. Maybe you should do him and get him out of your system, you know?" I thought about it.

"I don't know, Candy, I bet he would be amazing. I probably wouldn't ever want it to end." She laughed at me then spoke.

"OR he could be like those other guys where you thought it was going to be awesome, and it ended up being a disaster. Like Tiny Dick Dominic, sexiest man I have ever seen with a little thingy." We both laughed for a while over that.

Then we heard a noise coming from outside. We both ran, well practically tripped over each other to get to the window facing my sexy neighbor's house. As we squished our faces up against the window, we both gasped. "OH.MY.GOD. SCAR," was all she could say.

Darien was out in his back porch fighting a punching bag. I thought I heard tools going on this afternoon; he must have just put it up. He was a sight of pure masculinity. This was the first time I had seen him shirtless, and even in the dim porch light I decided he should do it more often. Who needed shirts anyways? I looked down. Well, I do, but that's beside the point.

He punched that bag with precision hits. He was so beautiful the way he moved. It wasn't choppy; it was almost like a dance. I could stare at him doing this all day. I sighed. Candace sighed along with me.

"Scarlet, you need to tap that, like stat. I mean, look at that body." I was. He was so beautiful. I could see the sweat glistening in the light, which made me think of how I wanted to get all sweaty with him in bed. I groaned then trudged back to the couch and sat my butt down. Sulking.

"I am so screwed." She came over and hugged me. "Not yet, sweetie, but if I were you I would be begging to get screwed by that." I giggled, oh Candace.

"Tell me about you and Ross, I feel like I've been rambling on about Darien, and you have actually been getting some. Details." She filled me in on the details, how great he was, how sweet he was, how much he enjoyed sports like her. I was really happy for her that she has someone that is making her happy. Everyone deserves to be happy, right? So maybe I shouldn't fight whatever it was between Darien and me. She started telling me about how his family has a cabin in the mountains of West Virginia, and that we should all go out there together. It sounded like fun; I hadn't been around the mountains in a while.

About an hour later, we said our goodbyes and made a plan to go dancing tomorrow night after I got back from Darien's parents' house. After watching her leave, I looked over next door. I turned around and walked upstairs to get ready for bed. After taking a shower, I crawled into bed.

I slept ok; I think my body craved the nook. My body and mind were already addicted to him. I got up and walked downstairs to let the dog out and filled up her bowl. I went back inside to fix a cup of tea when my phone beeped. It was a text message from a number I didn't recognize. It said,

My nook was feeling very lonely last night. —Darien.

I couldn't hold the grin off my face. I missed his nook too. I typed back,

Poor little old nook, will it survive? ;)

It could use a little loving. ;) ;)

I bet it could use a cold shower instead. :P

Didn't help. : (

What time are we heading out?

I'll pick you up around 2:00, sound good? It's not that far away.

Cool, I will see you then. :P

Yes, you will.

I went back to my morning routine with a big smile on my face. My mood for the rest of the day was fantastic. After work I came home, took a shower, and then tried to decide on what to wear. I decided on a pair of jeans and a nice long sleeve sweater than showed my shoulders. I put on a little makeup and my necklace. I braided my hair off to the side to show off my shoulders more. One glance in the mirror and I decided I looked cute. I walked down the stairs just as Darien knocked on the door. I went over and opened it. He stood there in all his sexiness wearing jeans slung low and a buttoned up green shirt. He looked at me from my toes up. He coughed then spoke.

"You look amazing. Ready to go?" I nodded and said goodbye to Roxy. I made sure she was set up with a nice bully stick to keep her entertained for the rest of the day. I grabbed my stuff and we headed over to Aunt Tara's Jeep. "She left you the Jeep too huh? Nice."

"Yeah, since I've been a Seal I haven't needed a car, so it was pretty cool of her to leave it to me." We talked through the thirty minutes to his parents' house. We pulled into a driveway of a very beautiful two-story brick house with blue shutters.

"It's so beautiful." He smiled at my approval. We parked, got out and walked up towards the door. Beautiful roses lined the sidewalk to the door. It smelled so good. I just wanted to pick a flower from each bush to put in a vase back home. As soon as we knocked, a beautiful black haired woman opened the door. She had to be related to Darien, they looked so much alike.

"You'll need to lay off the steroids, little girl, before they kick you out of the Girl Scouts." That was one hell of a hello.

"Sammy, good to see you too." Sammy laughed and jumped to hug Darien.

"Punk! I didn't know you were in town! When did you get home?" she squealed, then pulled back and smacked him on the arm. "I just got in a few days ago. I needed to settle in the house before I came here." She nodded like he meant something else.

"Well I'm glad you are back." She finally noticed I was there and her eyes widened, then she threw her hand out to introduce herself.

"Hi there, I am Samantha, Darien's big sister." I took her hand gladly. "Scarlet Barnette, his neighbor." She looked at Darien then back to me and smiled.

"Well, come on in, you guys, Mom just took out some goodies." She turned and walking into the house somewhere. "Yeah, this is going to be fun," Darien said as he shoulder bumped me then gestured for us to walk inside.

Inside his family's house was very comfy. It felt like a happy family lived here. Beautiful leather couches with patchwork quilts hanging on the backs. Pictures plastered to every wall. I hadn't even met the family besides the sister and I already could tell they loved each other more than anything.

"Mom, you are never going to guess who just walked in the house," Samantha says around the corner.

"Who? Is it that girl next door asking about our boy again? She needs to give up already." I giggled then looked at Darien, he just shrugged. As we rounded the corner, a woman, that I guessed was his mom, screamed. She stopped what she was doing and ran over to hug him and then smacked him on the arm. Goodness he was going to have one bruised arm after this visit. I couldn't help but laugh about it though.

"How come you didn't call your mother? I always worry to death about you!" He cowered a bit.

"Geez, Mom, I had to get settled before I came over for your abuse," he teased.

"Oh poppy cock, you could have called your mother." He shrugged and gave up.

"You're right, but I'm here now. What are you cooking?" She walked over and opened the oven. Bless this woman's heart. I think I love her.

"Is that a carrot cake?" I asked. She nodded and said, "Yes, ma'am, it is my specialty. I'm so sorry, hon., I forgot to introduce myself. I am Olivia, this little devil's mother." I just waved. "I'm Scarlet Barnette, his new neighbor." Recognition grew in her eyes, then they glazed over with a glassy sheen. She came over and hugged me.

"Oh, Scarlet, I have heard so much about you from Tara. You have no idea how much I appreciated you being there for her." When she pulled back, tears looked to be brimming her eyes and at any moment they would spill over.

"Thank you, she was a really kick-ass old lady," I said. She laughed and walked away. It looked like she wanted to compose herself from getting too emotional. My mom got like that too. She always wanted to be strong for everyone.

A high pitched squeal came from the stairs, a little child about five years old and a toddler came running full speed towards Darien. "Oh no! The little heathens!" Darien took off towards the living room area and let them tackle him on the couch. It was very amusing seeing him play around with them. My chest tightened at the sight. I envisioned him playing with his own kids like this. He would be the perfect family man. I had to look away before I started dissecting that thought. His sister came over and started conversing with me.

"So you got a thing for my brother, huh?" I knew this would come up. I never told a lie and I didn't plan on it now, but I also was not going to confess how deep I was in.

"He is pretty cool," was all I said. "Yeah, he is pretty cool." Then a little louder she said, "Especially when he watches my kids so I can have a date night with my husband." Darien chuckled from the room. I watched as he whispered something into the kids' ears with a shit eating grin on his face.

Then suddenly the kids scrambled off of him and ran at me screaming. It was terrifying! His sister laughed. "Oh, sorry, sweetie, even I can't save you now." I took off running towards the couch as well so I would have a soft landing when they got me. Little arms grabbed my legs and I just barely missed the couch and hit the floor. Damn, I thought I had that in the bag.

CHAPTER 10

DARIEN

Scarlet was officially the most graceful, clumsiest person I knew. When my niece and nephew took her down, I knew she was aiming for the couch but totally missed. I laughed so hard I thought I was going to piss my pants. Scarlet was looking at me like she might attack me if I kept laughing. I introduced them to Scarlet. My five-year-old niece, Riley, then screamed "let's get him!!" They all joined in on trying to tickle me. I got a hold on Riley and tickled her sides. She was the most ticklish there. The littlest one, Alex, was two so I let him get away with thinking he was tickling me, I laughed and screamed for help.

Scarlet decided to go for the kill and actually tickle me. Her feminine hands grasped the spot between my ribs and hip. My hips bucked, my fake scream for help turned into a real one, and I had to get off that couch. I grabbed Riley and threw her over my shoulder and took off running. Scarlet grabbed Alex and headed after us.

I stopped behind Sammy. "Big sister, I need your protection." She laughed and grabbed Riley then pushed me towards Scarlet and Alex. Alex squealed in joy. Scarlet laughed. I swear nothing hit me in the chest more than seeing Scarlet laughing with my family, and holding my nephew. Sights like that would kill you. I couldn't get the image of her with a kid out of my head. She would be the coolest mom ever. Just then my mom came back and thankfully interrupted my thoughts from going further.

"Alright, children, let's go have some cake." Scarlet set Alex down and the kids ran off towards the table. We all walked over and sat down. Scarlet and I kept stealing glances at each other. As she took bites of her carrot cake she would moan slightly, and the things it did to me. Damn it, fourteen-year-old Darien was back, sitting right in front of my family for Christ's sake. I had to shift to make room for big D down there. Yeah,yeah. I call him big D. It's the best name in the fucking world.

"So, Scarlet, Tara told me you had your own... How did she put it? Kick-ass studio," Mom asked. The grownups laughed.

"Yeah I kick ass in my studio. I own a business called Scars. I teach self-defense and kick boxing. I feel it's really important for people to know how to defend themselves." She was always so proud of her business, and she should be.

"That is very cool," Sammy said. Mom looked at us and I could see her trying to see us together. I knew she would be a little forward with me bringing Scarlet here. "Darien, how are you settling into the house?"

"I love it. Trying to man it up a bit. Just ordered a few things, you know flat screen, the works." Mom laughed. It was nice seeing her laugh; I know she was having issues with Aunt Tara passing. They were ten years apart, so they didn't really get close until after mom graduated high school. They became best friends after that. We had an endless amount of conversation flowing. Every once in a while, Sammy or Mom would try and bait us to see if we were together, but we told them we were just friends. Which, might I add, is awesome to hear Scarlet say I was her friend; one step closer to having her as mine.

After a few hours with my family we decided to head out. Dad was working, so I didn't get to see him. But I promised I would come back another day this week and that I would call first. On the ride back I broke the silence first. "Thank you for coming with me, you really helped lighten the mood a lot." She looked at me, like she was very happy to have been helpful.

"It was no problem, I had a great time. Plus, I can never say no to carrot cake." She giggled. She was too freaking cute. Carrot cake, I would buy her that shit everyday if I got to hear the noises she made when she ate it. Oh god, it was so hot.

Once we got home I walked her to her door. She stopped and looked at me. "Thank you again for inviting me, I had a nice time." She turned towards me.

"It was awesome, thanks for going. What are you doing tonight?" She smiled, god, I love that smile.

"Candace and I are going out tonight, going to have a girl's night. You?" Girls night, huh?

"Ross and I were thinking about going out for a beer." She moved a bit closer. I felt a little paralyzed, had she changed her mind?

"Well I hope you have fun." She started fiddling with her keys. Wait! Shit I saw this movie. Hitch, where he says if a chick fiddles that means she wants a kiss. Fuck yeah! I want that so bad. My body was already coming to life over the thought of touching those lips again. I wanted to take that chance. I pushed back a piece of hair that had come into her face and curled it behind her ear. Those beautiful emerald eyes lifted, her face blushed, and her lips parted. I could tell she wanted this just as bad as I did. I leaned in and brushed my lips across hers. Her breaths grew more rapid and heavy. My heart kicked up, felt like it was going to burst through my chest.

My name came out on a whisper and I couldn't wait any longer. I pressed my lips to hers; her hands came to my arms and gripped. We continued the soft kisses, and then she pressed into me. Mashing her bountiful chest into mine, I deepened our kiss. Her body shivered, a little moan came from her lips. I ran my tongue over her lower lip; she parted giving me the access I needed. I sucked in her bottom lip, she tasted like heaven. Our tongues caressed each other.

GOD! I could do this all fucking night.

My hands ran over the curves of her waist, she felt so good in my hands. I slowly moved her up against the door; her body was trapped in between mine and the door. Her lips were so sweet, fitting so perfectly with mine. Much, much to my regret my Seal senses kicked in once I heard the bushes by her driveway move. I stopped the kiss and turned my back to her, while keeping my hands on her sides I scanned the yard.

"Darien, what is going on?" she whispered, sensing something off. My eyes narrowed, I saw nothing, but I knew something or someone was out there somewhere close. I turned back to her. "Nothing, I thought I heard something." I didn't want to freak her out. I would definitely be keeping more of a protective eye around our houses. "Oh, okay." I grazed my hand across her cheek.

"You should go get ready for your girl's night. Have fun." I was so hoping having fun in her eyes wasn't hooking up with some guy. Especially after that hell of a kiss! I was starting to think we were pulling back layers here. "Oh yeah, girl's night. Alright, will I see you tomorrow?" she asked desperately.

"Already wanting to see me again, huh?" She blushed, and I chuckled a bit. It made me thrilled to be affecting her so much. I softly kissed her again, needing my fix until tomorrow. "Goodnight." I started heading back out towards my house. She said goodnight but very softly and went inside. I glanced back to make sure she was inside and okay.

Now time to scope out what that noise was. I went into complete Seal mode and went over to those bushes. A few twigs were snapped, and the dirt had been moved around a bit. Someone was out here. But why? Were they watching me or Scarlet? Looks like I will not be getting much sleep for a while, it's going to be nighttime scoping for me. Knowing no one was around now, I headed back into my house. Everything looked okay, so at least no one tried to get inside. I texted Ross seeing what he was up to since he wanted to go out tonight. We decided to meet at a place called The Machine. My stomach growled. Food sounded pretty good. I went into the kitchen and found some leftovers and ate that while I waited till it was time to go.

The Machine was a pretty relaxed place where you just go hang out and have a beer or dance a little on the floor. They usually played all different types of music. Ross was telling me all about Candace while we were sitting with our drinks, when a female body suddenly was in my lap. I found the face of the body and groaned in disappointment.

"Hey, baby, I didn't know you were back in town. You should have called me! I would have welcomed you back properly." She wiggled in my lap, definitely not getting the reaction she was wanting. Normally a little play time with Randy would be just what I would want. She was one of the usual women that ended up in my bed while I was on leave. But not now. Now I wanted a tall, sexy brunette with emerald eyes, and nothing fake on her. Randy was a 5'4 fake blonde with just as fake boobs.

"Thanks, Randy, but no thanks. I'm not interested this time." She pouted those big lips at me.

"Baby, I wouldn't mind having another girl with you if you are already playing with someone else. It could be fun." She wiggled a little more. There was never anything more for me with her than someone to keep my bed warm. I was starting to get annoyed real fast. "Randy, it ain't going to happen. Now if you will excuse me I'm going to the bathroom."

I just got up and walked towards the bathroom to splash my face with some water. As I came out Randy was there and she just kissed me. Out of fucking nowhere! She tasted like whiskey and cherries. Fuck this.

I grabbed her arms and pulled her off me. "What the hell?" I growled. She just looked at me like she just gave me a winning lotto ticket. "Just showing you what you want. You'll call me." Then she sauntered off, swaying her hips triumphantly. I stayed there for a minute against the wall and just closed my eyes. Just breathing in and out, in and out.

I decided it was time to go back to my table when I saw a pair of emerald eyes meet mine before heading out the front door. FUCK! Hopefully she didn't see any of that shit with Randy. Ross was just sitting there where I left him.

"Hey, man, you missed Candace and Scarlet, they were having drinks here too." Well shit. She probably didn't miss Randy's little lap show and the kiss. Damn it. Ross continued to speak. "Candace was hot as hell, but Scarlet seemed a little off. I wonder what her deal was." Damn it.

"Maybe it was because she and I kissed today and she saw Randy sitting on my lap and the fucking kissing assault she gave me coming out the bathroom. Fuck, man, she's going to think I'm with Randy while trying to get with her." He laughed at me. Good old Ross, I'm screwed and he laughed. "Fuck, man." He laughs even harder. "Ass," I muttered.

CHAPTER 11

SCARLET

Of course he went out with another woman. He was so fucking hot, with his black hair and beach eyes. What the hell was I thinking about considering trying to take it to a more physical level? We became friends real quick, and with today's kiss, I thought things were going really smoothly. Then I see some big fake tits chick crawl in his lap! He didn't even do anything to get her off! Then they were kissing by the bathrooms, ugh how sick.

"You know, babe, you're speaking out loud, right?" Candace pointed out to me as we drove home together... Oops. "Sorry, I mean, we had such a great day today! Had a really wonderful kiss goodnight then some chick is all over him at the bar. I can't help it."

"Sorry, babe, I thought he was a good one too. Fuck him, you are a gorgeous bitch. You don't need his sexy ass." I groaned. "He does have a sexy ass."

She laughed and agreed. "Yeah, he does." We spent the rest of the ride home talking about his impressive rear. Once we got to my house I headed inside and went to bed. I really tried not to dream about Darien, but my mind just really wouldn't listen.

Roxy woke me up, thankfully not by licking me this time. I went through my morning routine on autopilot. I ended up at work, not remembering the ride over. I mean, was I really this messed up over him? It hadn't been that long. I knew I liked him, but come on. I needed to go out tonight and get my mind off Darien. I sent a quick text out to Candace before class started.

A few people showed up early, so I figured we would start with some stretching this morning. I loved stretching and doing yoga, I was starting to feel good already. Ross strolled in again today; he had been so helpful these past couple days of class.

"Hey, Scarlet, how's it hanging?" I laughed; he had a way of doing that. "To the left today." It was his turn to chuckle. Everyone got geared up and was ready to go.

Class went smoothly and an hour later everyone was heading out. I had another class in about an hour. I felt like I needed to go a few rounds with the punching bag, I had enough time. I wrapped my hands with tape and started round one with the bag. I loved this. I wasn't able to actually fight with many people around here so this was my next choice. My fists were flying at full speed. My kicks were perfect! I was at it for about thirty minutes when the bell on the door rang and Darien walked in. Shit. I was going to try avoiding him. He sent me a few texts, of course which I said nothing back. I just didn't quite know what to say. Once I thought about it, even though we kissed, he wasn't mine.

"Hello," I said, very professionally. "Hey, Scarlet, you're a really good fighter. I just saw the last piece of it, but very precise." Starting off with flattery won't win me over, punk.

"Oh, thanks, I love what I do." I walked over and grabbed some water and a towel. He came closer. "So I came here because I wanted to talk to you." I kind of wanted to talk to him, but kind of not. OH, LIGHTBULB!!

"Ok, I will talk with you, if you spar with me. You're the only person I've met so far that is equal." He grinned. "Sure, I need some practice anyway." Perfect, I can get things off my chest and kick his ass a bit. We faced each other, both of us ready for an attack.

"Why are you avoiding me, Scarlet?" he started, and then rushed over with a right, left, right jab. Which I deflected. "I needed time to think about what to say." I went with a low kick trying to throw off his center of gravity, he jumped and I missed.

"So I am guessing you saw me last night. Shit, I knew it. It wasn't what it looked like." Both of us were kicking and throwing punches but none of them landing. I was starting to feel better already.

"So you kiss me then have some fake tits blonde giving you a lap dance and just happened to fall on her mouth?" I juked and faked a hit to the right but hit him with my left in the shoulder. HIT! Finally!

He rubbed his shoulder then came at me again. "That isn't what happened. Randy was one of the girls who normally I would play around with while on leave, but she sat on me and I told her it wasn't going to happen and left for the bathroom. She assaulted me once I came out and I pulled her back immediately. You got to believe me. I really like you and I'm not a bed jumper."

We went back and forth for a few minutes without saying anything, just trying to find a weak spot in our defenses. Finally, he got my legs while I was shifting positions and I went down to the mat. He pinned me real quick.

"Scarlet, you've got to believe me. I would never do that to you." I did believe him. Maybe it was a mistake. I didn't know, but I did believe him.

"I believe you." I snaked my leg around his and flipped him under me, changing up who was pinning who. He looked impressed. "So all is forgiven?" Not the puppy eyes!!! Stupid lethal puppy eyes.

"Yes, all is forgiven." He grinned so cheesy. "Thank god, I have wanted to do this all day." He pulled me down and kissed me. Mmm, despite thinking he was the devil earlier I would have kissed his sexy lips in a heartbeat. He heard my moan and growled. So masculine, so... just so yummy!

My body hot already, intensified. My blood felt like lava, and my heart was going like a hummingbird. He tasted like spice, man, and a little salt, but damn was it delicious. My hips moved on their own trying to find a little friction to help with the pressure building in my core. His hands left me and went to my hips pressing them into his more. *GOD*! He was hard.

We were moving together, against another while exploring each other with our mouths. I could tell I was getting close. That glorious cliff I wanted to throw myself off of was just there, I could see it. I ground myself more on him, not leaving a centimeter between us. I gasped.

He growled again. "Fuck, Scarlet, you are so fucking good, I want to bury myself inside you on this floor. Make you scream as you clench that sweet pussy around my dick. I bet you taste sweet as honey, baby. I can't wait to taste you." Oh god, my insides clenched at the sounds of his words. I loved a man who did dirty talk. It was so hot hearing what he wanted and how. We were devouring each other. I haven't ever done anything sexual at work but I was five seconds from changing that.

A cough broke through my lust. We stopped abruptly and looked towards the noise. Ross. "As much as I love a good show, I don't think you guys would want the next class to see your exhibition." He chuckled. We snapped away from each other so fast. Thankfully as people filled into the room we were a pretty good distance away from each other. My face was probably flushed, my lips were that amazing kissed swollen. I tried smoothing myself out more. I looked over at Darien and I laughed. His back was turned towards me, pretending to read the posters on the wall. I knew he just didn't want people to see his very manly bulge in his jeans. Poor guys, you can always see their lust. I giggled and decided I might as well use him.

"Good morning, class! Hope you guys had an awesome week, today we are going to work on those upward thrusts, and some combo moves." The guys went to put on their helmets and gear. I walked over to Darien.

"Go put on your gear, sailor. You're going to be my dummy today." I winked at him and smacked his butt as he walked away. He laughed then went to put everything on. We practiced thrusting our heels into our attacker's nose, then the classic combo S.I.N.G. Solarplex. Instep. Nose. Groin. Darien was the perfect dummy for this. I got to beat him up and he couldn't do anything back. HA!

We all went out for our weekly drinks at Parkers afterwards. Candace and Ross could not keep their hands off each other. It was kind of cute.

"So what do you think, guys? Scarlet and I were thinking about going dancing tonight. You guys should come with us. You know, protect us poor defenseless females." Candace pouted as she spoke. She was really trying to lay it on thick with them. Ross yelled, "Hell yeah, babe, any excuse for you to rub that sexy ass against me I am down!" She wiggled against him, I guess giving him a preview. I needed to let go, and just let the rhythm take me. Darien bumped his shoulder into mine.

"I'm down for that." He winked. I take it he wanted a little ass wiggle too. I winked back. He smiled, he was really cute. I honestly do believe him about that girl. I had watched a lot of girls eye him tonight and he never once showed any interest. And they were waiting like vultures for me to go to the bathroom or anything to swoop in and take him.

We made plans to go out, but us girls wanted to go get changed into something nicer. Candace and I decided to go to my house and get dressed while the boys did whatever, and then we would meet up at Fireflies, the fun dance spot in town.

Once we got inside, I took care of everything with Roxy and we headed to my closet. It was a chilly night so I would definitely need a jacket. "Okay, what should we wear tonight? Something sexy for sure," Candace said while staring at my closet. She pulled out a blue dress.

"How about this for you? You look hot in it," she said. "Nah, too chic. I want something a little more for dancing, you know? I can't move in that as much." She pondered what I said then she pulled out a burgundy quarter sleeve dress. The hem came just above my knee.

Perfect, it was a nice cotton dress so I would be able to dance and breathe.

"Perfect! Now it's your turn." I ran over to the closet and picked out something nice for her. We had a few clothes that could fit each other at my house, thankfully. She liked the yellow dress I picked and we finished getting ready and headed out to the lounge.

We walked into Fireflies and saw the music was in full swing, people were getting their groove on, and it was awesome. We found a little table by the bar and set our jackets down. The bartender, Tony, was a good friend of Candace's, so we walked over and he hooked us up with some drinks. She held her shot out, "Love you, bitch!" she yelled. We clinked glasses and downed that calming liquid. I could feel my body begging to be on the dance floor. "Come on, let's dance!" I yelled, as I grabbed her hand and led her to the floor.

The bass of the music was thumping in my veins. I loved to dance, just letting your body take over. And that's exactly what I did. I closed my eyes, lifted my hands to the ceiling and started to move. Rolling my hips, my head moving with the rhythm. Hands folded around mine above my head. I knew who exactly it was, Darien. No other person could make my toes curl with just a touch, or smelled as good as him. His breath was at my neck.

"You move like a goddess," he whispered into me. Keeping my rhythm and my eyes closed I kept dancing with him. Just letting our bodies move as one. I leaned my body into his and snaked my hips from side to side against his hard body. His hands ran down my arms, my sides, and the curves of my waist to grab those hips, to bring them closer. He growled at the contact. I felt the hardness in his jeans, goose bumps covered my body. He lightly moved his lips up my neck towards my ear. "Damn, Scarlet, what are you doing to me?"

I bit my lip and turned around. I opened my eyes and damn, he was so beautiful. I ran my hand through his thick black hair and down to graze his stubbled jaw. His eyes grew with hunger. I could see he was battling himself, against what, I couldn't tell. I couldn't think of anything else but him.

I wanted to devour him, consume him, to have him. His grip on my hips tightened. He leaned in so close I could feel his breath on my lips.

"What do you want, Scarlet?" What did I want? I wanted him, I needed to have him.

"I want you, Darien." He closed the distance between us, this kiss was unbelievable. So much need, passion. I needed more!

"Darien," I gasped. His hands tightened. "I know what you need, baby, come with me." He took my hand and led me towards the back hallway. I had never been back here before; it just looked like a bunch of offices. He opened one. Thankfully there was no one in there. I couldn't wait any longer, and I needed something, anything from him.

He closed the door after we walked in and locked it. Two seconds barely passed before we were clawing for each other. "Fuck, Scarlet, you are so fucking beautiful," he said in between kisses. He walked us back until we hit a desk. He wrapped his hands around my thighs and set me on top of the desk and moved between my legs. His hands felt so delicious, slowly taking time to move the hem of my dress up, and up.

Finally settling his hands on my bare hips. Our kisses grew frantic, his mouth moved to my neck. My hands came up his back to his head. I needed to grip something. He let out a rough breath and continued to move his mouth and tongue around my neck, and collarbone. His hands moved from my hips up to touch just below my breasts. I arched my chest in anticipation. My nipples pebbled and ached, waiting for his touch. He slightly bit where my neck and shoulder meet and brought his hands to where I wanted them now. His hands grasped my breasts, kneading them. It felt so good.

My body was wound up so tight I needed some release. His thumbs rubbed over my nipples, and tweaked them, I shuddered a moan. "God, Darien, that feels so good, but I need... I need."

He cut off my stumbling around for words with a fire hot kiss. "I know, baby," he spoke against me. His hands traveled back down my body, one gripped my waist, and the other kept on going down. His fingers lightly touched over the lace, and grazed over my sex. I knew he could feel what he was doing to me. He groaned and moved my panties aside and parted my wet folds.

"Fuck!" His mouth clashed with mine. He moved his fingers up and down, and then circled over my clit, sending shivers all over my body.

"Babe, you're so fucking wet, all of this for me?" My hips moved forward, aching for release.

"Darien, it's all for you. Please." His mouth came back to mine, we moved against one another. He entered his waiting fingers inside me. Jesus H Christ! It was so much! My senses were in overdrive! He immediately started moving in and out, curving right at the sweet spot. His thumb pressed on that little bundle of nerves. I couldn't help the moans and sounds that were coming out of me.

My body flushed with pleasure. I felt myself climbing up that cliff. My muscles tensed. He kept his relentless pace, sweetly pushing me closer and closer. Until I fell and I fell hard.

I cried out into his mouth. Stars exploded in my head. My insides clenching as my orgasm hit me. This was amazing!

Darien never let up and kept going until I was gracefully coming back to the world. He started to slow our kisses. His pace slowing and finally he withdrew his fucking amazing fingers. "OH. MY. GOD," was all I could say. His smug expression showed me he knew that he just rocked my world, and, Jesus, how much he rocked my world.

CHAPTER 12

DARIEN

She owns me. That's all there was to it. Feeling her coming apart with my hands was pure fucking amazing. Her lips were swollen from our kissing, her face was flushed from what we did. I didn't want any other fucker in this place to see how she looked after she fell apart like this. She was amazing. I was in love with this woman. She owned me. Period.

I wanted to take her right here, against this desk, just bury myself inside her to the hilt. But I wanted to take my time with her. Worship her the way she should be, and I couldn't do that here. I pushed a piece of hair out from her face. I brought my fingers that were inside her to my mouth. I was right, she tasted so sweet. I couldn't wait to have more.

"You taste delicious. I can't wait to make you come with my mouth." Her eyes rolled back, a very soft moan came from her throat. I continued, "But not here, baby. I want to take my time with you, lick every inch of your body." She grabbed me by the shirt and crushed her lips to mine. I guessed she liked my dirty talk. Her body shuddered and invaded my mouth, leading her tongue over mine. Tasting herself on me. God, that was so fucking hot! I stopped us before I lost control.

"Okay, we need to go back out there before I say fuck it and take you here against this desk." She nodded.

We walked back out to the dance floor, and no one looked at us. Good, I wouldn't want her to feel embarrassed if she thought everyone heard what we were doing. Candace and Ross were dancing in the middle of the floor. I led us over and joined them. We danced and laughed. Somehow this woman dancing with me has turned one of the worst times in my life into the best times. I thought I was going to go crazy on this leave, and now I'm not so sure I want it to end. I needed to think about all of that, but not now.

Now I needed to make this woman mine. Her ass wiggled against me. My hands coasted her waist, I just wanted to fucking ravish her. I ran the tip of my nose along the side of her neck, and pulled her close. Her breathing grew heavy. I knew she could feel how hard I was for her. She ran her hands up my neck and through my hair. I loved it when she did that. It made me want to possess her, go fucking alpha caveman on her. That seemed like all I've wanted to do to her since I met her.

Candace came over and grabbed Scarlet from my grasp. "Oh my god, Scar! Ross just invited us to go to his family's cabin in West Virginia next week for a few days. He says there is supposed to be awesome skiing weather then. Please, please, please say you will go!!!!" she begged Scarlet, throwing out puppy eyes of her own. I wondered if that's what my puppy eyes looked like. It was a wonder Scarlet could say no at all to her.

"Sounds like fun." She looked at me. "You're going too, right?" I couldn't help the smile from creeping up on my face.

"Of course, I would love a little time on the mountain, their cabin is very secluded you know." I winked at her. Her eyes fluttered, and it looked like she shivered a bit as well. I loved that I affected her so much. I couldn't wait to have her underneath me. Candace shrieked, "Yay! I cannot wait!" Then she ran over to Ross, I guess, to share the joyous news.

"So, Darien, do you have any plans tonight?" Her mischievous smile made my dick throb.

"I was thinking about having a sleepover. You know, eating ice cream, listening to music, staying up all night, long hot showers, and sleeping in the same bed. You?" She bit her lip, and damn if that wasn't sexy as hell.

"That sounds amazing, care if I join you?" I just mentally fist pumped in the air, Scarlet wanted me for real. I inched closer to her and brought my hands to cradle her face. Her eyes looked up into mine. I could feel her willing me to say yes.

"Wouldn't be a sleepover without you." I leaned in and kissed her. I could feel her kiss down into my soul. Burning hot lust boiled in my blood. She whispered against me, "Let's get this party started." I was so down for that.

We said our goodbyes to our friends. Scarlet rode with Candace so she needed a ride from me back home, which I was happy to oblige. I put my hand on her lower back and led her towards the door.

"Valentine?" A shiver ran up my spine, and not a good one. Before I turned around I prayed it wasn't who I was thinking it was. Slowly and surely I turned around and saw the very person I didn't want to see.

"Fox," I said with a little bit of force. He looked just the same as the last time I saw him. He looked like trouble, sinister even with his gray eyes and blond hair. He had a long, jagged scar along his jaw. His eyes swept towards the woman next to me. *HELL NO!* I tucked Scarlet into my side. I wish I could just pull her into me to hide her from his gaze. And dammit if that gaze was pissing me off.

"Who's your pretty little friend?" he said with a provocative laced tone. "None of your business, Fox." I glared at him. He was a big guy, and the few times we had fought against each other, I always came out on top. But he liked to play real dirty. I didn't like that he was here, and paying attention to Scarlet.

"Of course." He raised his hands in surrender. Which wasn't like him. "It was my pleasure to meet you, sweetheart." He said sweetheart like it was the most delicious dessert he had eaten. She clinged a little tighter to me. He finally brought his gaze back to mine.

"Always nice to run into you, Darien. Still playing good boy scout I see." He was fucking with me. "Goodbye, Fox," I bit out, and turned us, then walked out of the bar. Putting as much distance as I could between Fox and Scarlet; he was bad news.

I turned up the heat as soon as we got in the car. It was damn cold outside tonight. She didn't mention that whole scene with Fox, and which I was happy with. I didn't want to talk about him. I pulled the car out of the parking lot and started our journey home.

"So Navy Seals are supposed to have like super control right?" she asked. My right eyebrow rose at her question. Odd.

"Yes, we have been trained to have superior control." She looked deep in thought for a minute, seeming to ponder over my answer. And then she sat on her knees and brought her mouth to my neck. *HOT DAMN!* Her tongue swirled, licked, and suckled. I groaned.

As her relentless assault on my neck continued I barely noticed that she had undone the buttons on my shirt. I had to keep my eyes on the road. I had control, I could do this. Her mouth started to travel south over my collarbone, circling my nipple, she lavished it then bit a little. I couldn't help the sudden intake of breath.

"Fuck, Scarlet, you're pressing that control of mine." I could feel her smile against me. She continued to lick and kiss her way down my abs to the top of my jeans. She wouldn't. Would she? She started unbuttoning my jeans. I growled "Scarlet," I said in my warning voice.

Too late.

She popped open my jeans, my dick sprang free from its denim prison, and before I could say anything more she had her perfect mouth on my dick.

"FUCK, BABE!"Must. Keep. Eyes. On. Road. She was twirling her tongue along the head, moving those rosy lips along my shaft. I knew if she kept this up I was going to blow. My head came back against the head rest. I could do this. I could get us safely home. The warmth of her mouth was consuming me. She kept going like it was the sweetest lollipop she ever tasted. Damn, she was so hot. Her head bobbed up and down as she fucked me with her mouth. I've had a lot of blowjobs, and Scarlet blew them all in the dust. I wanted to bow down to her and give her whatever she desired.

My hips started rocking with her movements, and she hummed with her approval. Shivers broke out over me. She was taking all of me like a fucking champ. My hands tightened around the steering wheel. Almost home I kept chanting to myself.

We pulled into the driveway in record time. Thank god! I pulled her head up from my dick and kissed her with everything I had. She hummed in delight.

"Is everything taken care of at your house? Do you need a few minutes?" She shook her head and continued to kiss me. She licked my lip and sucked on it. Fuck it. I buttoned my jeans real fast, rushed out of the car and scrambled to her side. I threw open the door and picked Scarlet up and carried her. She shimmied down my body and kept her mouth on my chest as I unlocked the door.

My body was wired. I felt like I would explode out of my skin if I didn't have her soon. As soon as we were inside I grabbed her ass and hauled her up against me. Her legs wrapped around my waist. I pinned her between the wall and me.

My dick was throbbing feeling how hot she was. I could feel how wet she was through her panties. My hands ran all over her, kneading her lush breasts. They fit perfectly in my hands, I firmly grasped them. She moaned, and I loved that sound. Without letting her down from the wall, I lifted that dress over her head and threw it to the floor. She was gorgeous. I brought my attention back to her mouth. She was eager. I wanted to slow things down but I didn't think I could. Round two I would take my sweet time with her. But right now, NOPE!

I pressed my erection into her lace-clad sex. She moved her hips, wanting that sweet friction. She pushed my shirt the rest of the way off. I needed her stat.

I got a good grip on her and headed up the stairs with her legs still wrapped around me. I kicked open the door to the bedroom and fell with her onto the bed. Her hands raked down my back, I arched my hips into hers. I brought my mouth down onto hers as we continued to get rid of our clothing. Once I had her bra unhooked and on the floor, I ran my tongue down to those precious globes of goodness. Rosy pink nipples tightened, swirling my tongue over its peaks, I softly sucked. Her hands gripped my hair, her hips rising towards mine. I switched my mouth to the other perfect, waiting breast to lavish the same treatment. She gripped me and brought my lips back to hers. Her hands ran down my chest, my stomach, and fiddled with the button on my jeans. She got it undone and ran her hand over my pulsing cock. I groaned in her mouth as I thrust into her hand. Fuck me, man, I had never been this turned on in my life!

She started pushing down my jeans and my boxers along with it. I got it the rest of the way off. I started kissing my way down to her lacy panties and very slowly gripped the sides and pulled them off her. Tracing my path with my tongue, I kissed my way back up her leg, then the other leg. There was no way I was not touching my lips to any part of her body.

"Baby, please tell me you are on birth control. I want to feel you surrounding me." She nodded then scrambled to grab me and bring me back up to her lips. I settled between her legs, positioned at her entrance.

She whimpered, "Darien, please." This was what I had been waiting for, making her mine. I slowly entered her inch by inch. She gasped. My body tensed, she felt so fucking good, so wet, and tight. I took slow breaths trying to keep from embarrassing myself. Finally, I was fully inside her. I stayed still to let her get accommodated to me. Her tight muscles started to relax, her hips moved to fully meet mine. I pulled back and look into her eyes.

"So gorgeous." I slowly pulled out to the tip, and then pushed back in. Her eyes rolled back into her head. Her mouth parted, both of us were breathing very heavy. I crashed my lips back to hers as I set a faster pace. Her sweet sheath clenched around me as I pulled out and glided back in.

"Oh god, Darien! So... so... Oh god!" Yeah I totally felt like a king right now. I ran my hand down her body and grabbed her hips. She wrapped her soft legs around my waist, giving me a deeper angle.

"Fuck, Scarlet!"I growled out. She moaned as I picked up a more relentless pace, thrusting faster and harder. I felt her start to tense up underneath me. "Darien!" Her body exploded in spasms of her release. Milking me into my own. I groaned as she continued to cry out my name. Tension coiled low in my balls. I rammed back into her one last time as the best orgasm of my life erupted from me. I could barely move. She was still riding the waves of her own release as I finished mine.

After we came back down from our explosion, I fell on top of her, trying not to put all of my weight on her. Our breathing still heavy she said, "Wow." I huffed.

"Ditto." She chuckled. I get up onto my elbows to look at her. She looked completely satisfied, blushed cheeks and a darker shade of pink swollen lips. I reached up and stroked the side of her face as she stared up at me. I bent my head back down to kiss her, just sweet, tender kisses. Hoping that in these kisses she felt the fact that she owned me. I knew I needed to clean up and take care of her so I slowly pulled out. "Be right back." Then I shuffled over to the bathroom to clean up.

CHAPTER 13

SCARLET

I'm ruined. He had completely ruined me for other men. Completely. I relaxed in bed while he cleaned up. Shivers of ecstasy still ran through me like little lightning bolts. That was the most amazing sex I had ever experienced! He strutted back to bed, he was so sexy. Hard chest and washboard abs, I just wanted to run my hands over every inch of him. He was so impressive, and I just had that. I turned to my side to face him as he sat next to me. "So what's next on our sleepover agenda?" I asked. He gave me a wolfish smile.

"I was thinking a little dessert. Why don't you just make yourself comfy and I will go get us some." He winked and walked down the hallway and down the stairs to the kitchen.

Wow, I still couldn't believe how he possessed me like he did. I mean, mind blowing. He was so sweet and had a very good attention to detail. I snuggled into his comforter, so soft, and it smelled like him and our sex. I loved that smell. I hummed in delight.

"Am I interrupting anything?" Dairen was standing beside the doorjamb holding a big bowl with two spoons in it.

"Nope, everything just smells so good. Like you." He smiled, and I melted. He strode over to the bed, I sat up against the headboard as he handed me the bowl. Mm, Ice cream. He scooped a little in the spoon and held it in front of my mouth. I came closer and stuck my tongue out and licked the spoon before putting it in my mouth. Mm, French vanilla. I flicked my gaze to his. His eyes were dark and held so much heat in them. I picked up the other spoon and did the same to him. He closed his mouth over the spoon and I felt drenched already. My body was heating up again. I didn't think I would ever get enough of him. I just wanted as much as I could get.

"Lie down on your back," he whispered. My stomach turned to butterflies with the anticipation of what he had planned.

After lying down, he slowly and tantalizingly pulled the comforter down to expose my breasts and stomach. His eyes grew hungry, and not for ice cream. He scooped up a little bit of ice cream. My nerves were going crazy trying to figure out what he was going to do. He very slowly placed the backside of the spoon in the dip where my throat and collarbone met. Holy shit that was cold! I shivered. He moved the spoon over my chest, melted ice cream leaking out onto my skin.

Goosebumps rose over my body, my nipples hardened like diamonds. I was so excited! He continued to drag the spoon across my skin until he reached my navel. He let the rest of it fill my navel. He placed the spoon and bowl on the nightstand before leaning over me. He snaked his tongue over the spots where the melted ice cream saturated my skin.

"Mm, French vanilla." My body shuddered with pleasure. He licked and sucked every part where the ice cream was, then dipped his tongue into my navel and lapped up the rest of what was left of the ice cream. I let out a soft moan. This was amazing. I've never had a guy tease me so much. Usually it was BAM BAM and we are done. Not Darien. He was taking his time with me and I loved it! I needed more.

I sat up and straddled him, pressing his back onto the bed. "My turn." He smiled and raised his arms to rest his head on his hands.

"Do whatever you want to me." I gathered the bowl; most of the ice cream was starting to melt. I scooped up some and started my very own treasure map on his chest. I traced his pecs and every hard ridge of his stomach. I made a little down detour to the V then dumped the rest in his navel. He licked his lips in anticipation. I started at the top and worked my way over every hard muscle of his. I could do this all day, just explore his body. During my tongue exploration I noticed a scar on his left shoulder. I traced it with my fingers then kissed it.

"Where did you get this one?" It looked a lot like mine.

"A bad guy got me with his bayonet. I had to go through five months of rehab to get my shoulder back to normal range of motion." I kissed it again. Wishing I could take away all the pain he went through. I went back to ridding his skin of the delicious French vanilla that was clinging to him. Licking up every last drop, I could feel how hard he was beneath me. I never knew a guy that could go again so soon. But I guess he already blasted all of my expectations of what it was like with him. I decided to roll my hips over him, back and forth over his erection. He groaned, and brought his hands to my hips to press me into him further.

I know it was probably way past midnight and we should get some sleep, but I wanted this. I wanted to make this last all night. I pressed my sticky chest to his, skin against skin. His hands ran up my back, one hand came to the nape of my neck and pulled my mouth to his. He tasted of ice cream. It was so delicious as his tongue caressed mine. I bit and sucked his lower lip, he growled. I was completely soaked and he was so hard as I moved over him. His hip lifted to get more pressure. I lifted up and placed him at my center. Our gazes locked on each other as I sank down onto him. My body still shuddered trying to accommodate his size. He filled me like he was made for me. Slowly I rose up and came back down.

"Fuck, baby, you are so good." I liked it when he called me baby. I found a good rhythm to ride him to. He was thrusting his hips up to meet mine as I came down on him. We were perfectly in sync. I moved up and down, and back and forth.

As I moved on him, I found the perfect spot and I couldn't help myself to keep going until I was suddenly over that cliff again and came so hard on him. My insides clenched him; I could barely keep moving it was such an amazing orgasm. He sensed my need for assistance and grabbed my hips to continue moving me over him.

"Oh Darien!" My toes curled and my eyes closed with the intensity of this feeling. It was pure euphoric bliss. As the waves of pleasure started to decrease, Darien rolled over taking me with him so I was under him. He started driving into me, pulling my legs over his shoulders and "OH FUCK!"I screamed as I exploded again!

My feet pressing into his shoulders, toes curling, and his movements became frantic. This was so much. Every nerve in my body was going crazy from what he was doing to me. He rammed me harder and deeper than anything I could have imagined. He groaned out a slew of curses and incoherent murmurs as he came. Filling me with his warmth. I felt so claimed and I really wanted to be claimed by this man. My legs dropped from his shoulders, they felt like Jell-O. I felt amazing.

He leaned down and kissed me so softly. I could definitely get used to this. He rolled over to the side of me and pulled me in close, I nestled myself in his nook. "So what next?" he breathed out as he kissed the top of my head.

"A nice hot shower would be nice. I feel a little sticky," I said. "Okay, let's go get wet." He scooped me up and carried me into the bathroom.

He turned on the water without putting me down. Still carrying me he stepped into the spray of the shower. I pressed my lips to his wet neck. Water droplets were gliding over his body. I wiggled down from him and grabbed the soap. I wanted to wash him. I ran the soapy lather all over his amazing form. He really was a freaking god; no man is that perfect. He took the soap from me and returned the favor of washing me. Taking more time in a few areas, of course. I washed off the soap and turned around to see him staring at me like he wanted to eat me.

"You couldn't be ready to go again," I questioned him then I looked down and, oh my god, he was hard.

"Oh on the contrary, love, I don't think I will ever be done with you." I knew how he felt.

He ran his hands over my breasts, teasing me. Ah, I needed him again, now! He saw the fire in my eyes and pinned my body against the wall with his. The tiles of the wall were cool, but my body was on fire with need.

He lifted me up by my ass and impaled me against the wall. "Oh god, yes!"

I felt like a live wire, I could come at any second with him. He started driving into me. Fucking me against the wall. I've never been fucked before him and I already was addicted. I couldn't hold out any longer. My body shook and exploded right there on the wall. It felt like a damn earthquake was going off in my body. I cried out, well maybe screamed was probably more the word I would use. He shattered along with me, his body trembled. His cock pulsed as he came inside me.

I wiggled down his wet body before we fell. He pushed the hair out of my face and kissed me all over. I was beginning to love this part after sex. He doted me in loving kisses, and I soaked them all in.

We turned off the water and began drying each other off. Neither one of us said a word to each other. We didn't need to; it was a silent understanding of oh my god that was amazing. I went back and snuggled in his bed, he joined me. He wrapped his arm around me as I settled into my nook. Yes, I was claiming his nook.

"Oh wait, I said music too. Do you have your phone or iPod with you?" Hm thinking was a little hard at the moment, did I?

"I think I do in my purse downstairs." I got up and went to his dresser and pulled out a big T-shirt of his. He gave a very satisfactory groan as he took in the sight of me in his shirt.

"You look so fucking hot in my shirt." I did a twirl to give him a better view then ran downstairs to grab my iPod.

My purse was by the front door, right where I figured it would be. I grabbed the device and headed back to the warm bed. I handed him the device as he plugged it into a set of speakers. We settled back into each other as music slowly filled the room.

First Iris, from the Goo Goo Dolls came on. I was slowly starting to get tired as we lay there just listening to music. It was so comfortable. The next song that came on caught my attention. Kiss me by Ed Sheeran. I listened to the lyrics and was stunned. I loved this song but somehow now I found it very fitting. They were beautiful words for how I was starting to feel.

Ed sang about feeling like you were falling in love.

I wouldn't have believed it but I think I was definitely falling in love with this man. He was everything I needed and more. I knew I was creating my own heartbreak by falling for him. Too late now. I closed my eyes and listened to the rest of my song for him. He turned his head towards me and whispered in my hair. "I really like this song." I tried not to overanalyze what that could mean and decided to just enjoy this moment with him. He hugged me tighter and I felt loved. I drifted off into a peaceful sleep with those feelings.

Chapter 14

Darien

Even though I was exhausted from the previous events I still couldn't sleep. I didn't want everything that happened between us to be a dream and wake up. I held Scarlet as she fell asleep in my arms listening to a song I would say was my song to her after hearing it. I never wanted this to end.

Hours passed, light started to enter the room from the windows. She rested so soundly all night. Time to wake her up! I slowly rolled her under me and cradled myself in between her legs. I started kissing her sensitive neck, while dragging my hard cock across her wet center. I guess someone had a very nice dream. She started making sweet murmurs, her eyes still closed. I intertwined my hands with hers and brought them out beside us.

"If this is a dream don't wake me." Her words were laced with sleep. "This is real," I whispered into the spot behind her ear having more meaning than one. This was the real thing for me. She moaned and turned her head to find my lips. She tasted like sweet French vanilla; it was the only flavor I had wanted since I saw her. My body came to life, every touch felt like an explosion of blissful sensations.

Our kisses started off slow, and then started to grow into full on wanton. Seeing my shirt on her made me feel possessive, like she was mine. But it had to go. We moved around until I drew the shirt over her head, exposing her beautiful chest. She opened her eyes and we were staring at each other for what seemed like forever.

"Darien, I need you." That was what every man wanted to hear. I growled, and then entered her in one quick thrust. Her back arched off the bed. I bent down and brought my mouth to any part of her skin I could get. Gliding in and out, letting my body do what it wanted. Her head was thrashing from side to side as she moaned. I knew the feeling, I felt like thrashing around she felt so good wrapped around me. She wrapped her legs around me, taking me deeper. She was staring up at me through hooded eyes. She was exquisite. Her eyes glazed over as her sheath started its death grip on me. Fuck, I was lost. Her waves of pleasure crashed over her, I couldn't hold back any longer. We cried out together as our releases claimed us.

I lowered myself down and settled my head in between her neck and shoulder. Our breathing and heartbeats started to slow. "Now that was one hell of a wake up." We both laughed at her statement.

I rose to kiss her. "Do you want some tea? Breakfast?" She smiled that bring-a-man-to-his-knees smile at me.

"Tea sounds good. I'm going to have to go take care of Roxy soon." I kissed her quickly again.

"Alright, I'll go start you some hot water so we can get the day started." She grabbed my shirt again to put on. I was going to have to give her a few of them just so I could see them on her all the time. I shoved on a pair of sweats and headed down the stairs. I really enjoyed our mornings together. I got the water going and started the coffee pot. She sauntered down the stairs a few minutes later. She was definitely something.

"So I was thinking after breakfast I need to take Roxy for a walk, would you like to join me?" I'm glad she wasn't trying to end our time together after what all happened. I was nowhere near being done with her.

"Sounds good. What would you like for breakfast? I have eggs, cereal, and, um, I think that is it," I said as I looked through my cabinets. I really only ate eggs for breakfast most of the time. High protein.

"Umm... cereal sounds good." Nice. I grabbed a bowl and got her all set up with her tea and cereal. She sighed in contentment. We enjoyed our cereal together, afterwards I put on a shirt and shoes and we grabbed her stuff, and then walked over to her house so she could get dressed and grab Roxy. I'm glad there were no other houses by us; I would seriously hurt someone if they saw her walking to her house in just my T-shirt. She had to be cold though.

She unlocked the door, fed Roxy and ran upstairs to get dressed. Things felt so natural with her. I was just staring out her back door towards the shoreline when she came back down the stairs, dressed in jeans and a tight green sweater. My eyes raked over her. She was so beautiful.

"Okay, Roxy, let's go for a walk," she spoke to the dog. The dog ran out the door as we trailed behind after locking up the house. We were walking a lot closer than last time; well, a lot of things have changed. Could it really only have been a few days since our last walk. Our hands brushed against each other as we walked. I shrugged to myself. Why the hell not? I wanted to do everything with Scarlet, all that Notebook shit you see people do. I gently grabbed Scarlet's hand and held it, my thumb rubbing back and forth over hers. She looked at our joined hands, then to my face. Her eyes lit up, and I could tell she was trying to not make a big deal out of it but really she was happy. "Soo..." she said. "So," I said back. She giggled. I loved that sound. I yanked her arm lightly so her body ended up crashing into mine. She looked up at me with questioning eyes.

"I really enjoyed last night. I don't want it to end, as long as that is okay with you?" I asked her. She answered me by kissing me. *Thank god*! I wasn't sure what I would have done if she decided it was too weird or something and wanted to be done. I wasn't ready to make decisions about what would happen after my leave. I wanted to enjoy my time with this girl who owned me.

We walked for about thirty minutes, as we got back to her house I got a feeling of foreboding. I walked in front of her and peeked through the windows, nobody inside. She hadn't noticed me in Seal mode yet, so I played it off and let her unlock the door. She grabbed the handle to stick the key in and the door opened. She looked a little puzzled.

"I could swear I locked the door before we left." She looked at me, trying to confirm or deny. We did lock her door before we left for the walk. Someone had been in here and didn't try to hide that they were. What the hell? I instantly thought about how Fox made himself known to me the other day. It kind of had his feel to this. But he wouldn't have left any sign he was here. Unless he wanted me to know. I pushed that thought back. He had no reason to come after me for anything. I haven't had anything to do with that fucker since he got dishonorably discharged of duty. It had to be someone else.

"Let me go inside first and check everything out. Please stay out here by Roxy." I slowly opened the door. I checked all the rooms, all seemed clear. Nothing looked out of place to me. I was very aware of my surroundings, my senses on alert. Why did someone obviously break in, did nothing to hide it, and take nothing? All seems clear.

"Okay, everything looks clear, but come in and check all of your stuff to see if anything is missing." She looked nervous going in the house, like someone was going to jump out and get her.

After walking around, she said nothing was missing. Roxy did walk around sniffing everything. We used dogs for missions all of the time. She knew there was someone in here too, a different smell. Looks like whoever was creeping by the bushes has been upgraded to a threat on my list.

"Do you have any plans today?" Scarlet asked, taking me out of my thoughts. "I didn't have anything planned, thought about going over to my parents' again. You?" She shrugged.

"No, I was just going to hang out at home, clean up a bit." I didn't want her being alone at home until I found this fucker.

"You should come with me to my parents' house. You can bring Roxy if you want. I'm sure Mom would love to see her," I said hoping that bringing Roxy into it might make her join me.

"Sure, that sounds good." She looked around. I guessed she felt a little uncomfortable being here by herself. Good, I didn't want her here alone, plus more time to spend with her the better. She needed to do a few things around the house, and I needed to call my mom before we left. I headed back over to my house to change into something a bit nicer, and phoned my mom. She answered on the second ring. "Valentine residence."

"Hi, Mom," I say. She shrieked, my face scrunched up as I held the phone a bit further away. "My baby. How are you?" I chuckled to myself.

"Great, Mom. So I was thinking about hanging out there today for a bit. Is everyone home?" I heard kids squealing in the background so I guessed my sister was there.

"Yes, everyone is here. We were thinking about doing a nice lunch. You should bring Scarlet over too. She was really nice." I'm glad my mom likes her. "Yeah, I think I will. Okay then, I'm going to go, but we will be over in a little bit," I said.

"Alright, we will see you in a bit. Oh wait, before you hang up, would you mind picking up some ice on the way, dear?" she asked. "Yeah, we can do that." We said our goodbyes and hung up.

I changed into a pair of jeans and a black long sleeve shirt. I took a look in the mirror. I looked a little scruffy, I haven't shaved since I got in. Screw it. I wasn't going to shave now. I put on a pair of boots, grabbed my stuff, and headed out the door.

As I walk in to Scarlet's house, she was typing on her laptop. Very into whatever it is she was looking at. Her lower lip pouts out a little and I'm tempted to go over there and bite it. Tempting. She glances up and a smile grew on her face. The corner of my mouth went up in response.

"Everyone is at the house. We have to stop for ice on the way, whenever you are ready," I told her. She closed her laptop and sauntered over. "I'm ready," she said. It's been like only an hour since I kissed her and I felt like a magnet being pulled towards her. I grabbed her hand and pulled her into me. I skimmed my nose over hers, around her cheek, her jaw. She smelled delicious. I finally settled my lips over hers. Sweet kisses. She whimpered when I broke the kiss. She looked at me with such fever.

"Let's go before I take you back to bed and we end up not leaving the house at all." She nodded. We locked up everything, and then double checked that we have secured everything again. Roxy followed us and we all quickly got into the Jeep. We talked about stories from our past. Her trips with her parents on their expeditions, my stories of being beaten up by Sam when I was younger. Fun stuff.

We stopped off at a gas station on the way and grabbed the ice. I missed home a lot. It was kind of nice being able to drop in randomly. I took a little stroll down memory lane as we pulled into my family's house.

CHAPTER 15

SCARLET

Darien seemed to be staring off into space as we pulled into the driveway. I wondered if something was bothering him. I thought about the unlocked door earlier, I was almost ninety-eight percent sure I locked the door. But nothing even looked like it had been touched. Why would someone break in and not do anything? It gave me the creeps. It's not like I had enemies or anything, and Frank was in jail. Plus, knowing how crazy Frank is he would have just waited for me and done something right then and there. I shook myself out of that thought. There was no telling what he would do.

I looked over at Darien and leaned over to brush some of his hair behind his ear and graze my fingers across the sharp line of his jaw. He looked at me and shook himself out of whatever thoughts he was having. He turned his head slightly and kissed my hand that was cupping his jaw. Sigh, he was just too freaking cute. He nodded towards the house. We all got out of the car and headed towards the door. Roxy was really excited. We go for walks and I take her to parks, but she doesn't go over to people's houses often. most are scared just because she looks like a werewolf. Mmm, I loved the smell of those roses. His parents' house is so lovely, so homey. His mom opened the door before we even knocked. She must have been peeking out of the window or something.

"There you guys are, oh, and there is Roxy. I haven't seen her in so long." She knelt down and started petting the dog. If dogs could purr I think she would be doing it right now.

"Come on in, guys. Drop the ice off in the sink please, Darien dear," she cooed to us as she continued to pet the dog. Foxy Roxy was definitely going to get spoiled today.

Darien took the ice into the kitchen and I took a look around. Last time I didn't really get a look at anything in detail. There were pictures lining the walls that were calling my name. A lot of pictures of the grandbabies. Alex and Riley when they were little bitty babies. Cute. Samantha and Darien playing in the backyard when they were little. Darien was even cute as hell back then. Although he looked like a troublemaker. Arms snaked around my waist and a warm breath washed over my neck. I shuddered. I swear he could make me convulse just by being near me.

"I was pretty cute, huh?" he teased. I smiled.

"I don't see the cuteness, but I do see a troublemaker." He chuckled, skimming his nose up the lines up my neck. I could have purred. God, he affected me so much.

"I was cute and pure innocence." It was my turn to laugh; somehow I doubted he was a boy scout. His mother popped in, I guessed she was done for now petting the fur baby.

"Alright, you two, take it upstairs if you're going to be attacking each other in the living room." I blushed, how embarrassing for his mother to see us like this. I turn towards her trying to untangle myself from Darien's grasp but he just wouldn't let me go.

"Mrs. Valentine, was Darien a little troublemaker?" She was looking very happy seeing us together. It made me blush even more.

"Please call me Olivia, dear. And yes, he was a pain in the ass. Always getting in trouble with Ross, playing pranks on other kids, and getting in fights." She narrowed her eyes at him; guess she was remembering all the stuff he did. I looked up at him and raised my right eyebrow, waiting to hear him contradict it. He just rolled his eyes.

"I plead the fifth," he conceded. I giggled. His mother just rolled her eyes, threw her hands in the air and walked off towards the door to the back yard. Darien kissed my head, and then grabbed my hand to follow his mother's path.

Stepping out onto the porch I noticed they had a beautiful backyard. Very well put together. They had a little swing set that Riley and Alex were playing on, and a beautiful gazebo where Samantha and, I am guessing, his father sat. His sister waved us over.

"Hey, punk. Hey, Scarlet." She grinned at us. We walked over and sat at the table in the gazebo. They looked so much like their father. He got up and hugged Darien, a nice big bear hug, and then came at me.

"I'm Jenson Valentine, you must be Scarlet." I nodded. "Yes, sir." He pulled me into his bear hug. It was nice, but a bit hard to breathe for the moment I was in his arms.

"It's nice to meet you. We were just talking about that old broad, Tara's, house. Have you done anything with it yet, son?" he asked Darien.

We took our seats around the table then Darien launched into a conversation about what all he had done to Aunt Tara's house since he has been in it. Samantha leaned closer to me.

"So, you and my brother, huh? I thought you guys were just friends." She bunny eared the best friend's part. "Kinda." I blushed. She nodded then winked.

"Good, I think you guys complement each other well." We flew into conversation about work, and her kids while the guys talked about the last football season, and things Darien did while away. It was very easy with his family. Everyone laughed and messed with each other lovingly. Olivia brought out some sandwiches, fruit, chips, and drinks. This was nice. Darien's cell phone started to ring during lunch.

"Excuse me, I'll be just a minute." He stood and left for the house to take the call.

"So, Scarlet, how is business going?" Jenson asked. "Really well. I have a class graduating this week," I said.

"That is great. We do a lot of self-defense training in the force as well. Good stuff." I nodded and took a bite of my sandwich. It was one delicious sandwich. After finishing my bite, I spoke up. "Thank you for lunch and letting me hang out here with you guys." They smiled at me; I felt warmth from it.

"It is our pleasure, dear. It's nice to have finally met you. We heard a lot from Tara. Finally we have a face with the name. It's nice to see Darien so happy as well," Olivia said. I blushed again. I wasn't usually this easy to embarrass. I looked towards where he went into the house. I wondered what the phone call was about. I briefly thought about how all this will probably be coming to an end after he leaves for the Seals again, and I would be heartbroken. No more amazing sex, easy conversations, or lunch dates with these warm, loving, people. I sighed. Samantha reached her hand under the table and squeezed mine. I looked at her face. Her eyes were relaying what I was thinking. She was comforting me. I squeezed back. Maybe she and I would become friends. I think I would like that. She was fun, didn't take crap from no one. A lot like Candace.

Darien sat back next to me, startling me out of my thoughts. I looked at him. He showed no signs of bad news so that is good. He smirked. Stupid, cute, smirk. I just wanted to kiss it right off his face. "News from base, son?" Jenson asked. Darien looked around at everyone.

"Yes, actually that was Lieutenant Commander Austin. He wants me to help out at the base this week training new seals." Everyone nodded and said that was pretty cool. That was pretty cool. I hope he would still be able to go to the cabin this week. I was looking forward to it.

"I am still going to the cabin this week with you guys," he answered my thoughts. My inner self was doing a happy dance, pumping her hands in the air dancing around in a circle. I winked at him. Everyone carried on conversations about his work, the kid's school, Aunt Tara. It was a good day.

After spending a few more hours at the Valentine residence, we decided it was time to head home. I was getting kind of tired and kind of wanted to take a nice bubble bath. Hm, that idea was sounding great. Roxy really enjoyed her day too, playing around in the yard with Darien's niece and nephew. She got so much attention. She passed out in the back seat as soon as we got in the Jeep.

"I have to go by the base for a quick briefing of my duties tomorrow, do you mind if I just drop you guys off?" he said.

"Yeah, that's fine. I was just thinking how a bubble bath would be nice." He coughed and then cleared his throat.

"A bubble bath, huh? Sounds like fun. Is it okay if I stop by later once I get back?" I glanced out the window and bit back a smile. I was enjoying this a little much. I wanted to be around him all the time. Geez I was in deep.

"That would be nice," was all I said without giving away how happy I was that he wanted to spend more time with me. We rode back to the house just comfortably listening to music. He pulled into the driveway and gave me a quick, but oh so promising, kiss. Great, now my body is ready for sexy time and he has to leave. I huff a little. "Tease," I called him.

I opened the door, Roxy followed me out and towards the house. I waved to him as I unlocked the door. It was sweet of him to wait and make sure I was in safe, especially after the probable breaking and entering earlier. Weird no one took anything. It made me feel a little weird in my house. I'm glad I knew to defend myself like I did. It was still light out. I wanted to take a bath with all of my candles lit, so I would have to do something else for a while. I fed Roxy and made myself some tea. She passed out on the couch as soon as she was finished with her food. Poor dog, she really wore herself out. I think a good book sounded good. I walked over to my bookshelf to my collection. What did I want to read?

I just finished the Percy Jackson series. Great series, but I wasn't ready to read it again. Harry Potter? I could always go for that, but I think I am in the mood for something else. Obsidian? Perfect! I loved this book! Hot aliens, lots of banter, building sexual tension, and can't forget the alien fights! Yep, I mentally patted myself on the back for picking this one. I curled up on the couch with the dog and started reading about Katy Swartz and her hot neighbor. Sigh, I loved my book boyfriend, Daemon Black.

After the sun set, I made myself something to eat then decided it was my bath time. I got everything ready and turned on the water, pouring in my favorite bubble bath, salts, and whatever else I had in my basket of bath goodies. My cell phone started ringing. I ran back downstairs to grab it.

"Hello?" I hear a lot of static on the line. Creepy. "Hello?" I say again. Still no answer. Okay, this is a little weird. I'll try again, after that I am hanging up. "Hello? Anybody there?" I listen carefully.

"Hello, honey? Scarlet? Can you hear me?" Oh my god, it's Mom! "Mom! Oh my god, hey,Mom! Where are you guys?" I run back upstairs and turn off the water so it doesn't overflow while I talk to her.

"We are in the Valley of the Kings. I think we found another tomb. Oh it is so exciting, dear. How are you?" I missed my parents a lot. My mom was such a warm person, funny, and a little over eccentric sometimes. I guess you'd have to be like that to write books and deal with my dad. He wasn't as big of a free spirit that she was. She brought him out of the history books and made him live life.

"I'm doing really good,Mom. I miss you." The static is starting to get a little louder. "I miss you too, honey. Your dad misses you as well." The static is so loud I can barely hear her now. "Honey, I'm losing signal. I've got to go, but I will call you the first chance I get when we are back in town. I love you!" she says through the static. "I love you too,Mom. Tell Dad too!" We hang up after that.

I got up and lit my candles surrounding the soaker tub, undressed, and descended into the delicious, hot water. I could feel the knots in my shoulders melt away. So relaxing. I grabbed my phone to turn on some relaxing music. My phone beeped. Oh a text!

Is it too late to get all wet and bubbly in the bath? ;) Darien

I laughed so hard seeing this. Hm, yep time to tease.

I'm soaking wet. Oh god, these bubbles feel so good over my skin.

....

Ooo yeah I feel so soft. Mmm, Darien.

I'm coming over now.

OH I'm so close...

I'M GOING TO BREAK DOWN YOUR DOOR!

Or you could use the key under the gnome by the door. ;)

I heard a rustling noise downstairs and someone running fast up the stairs. I giggled. Guess he was in a hurry. He busted through the door in all of his naked and hard glory. I couldn't help from laughing.

"Did... you... run here naked?" I spoke through my laughter. He narrowed his eyes.

"No, but there is a bread crumb trail of my clothes back to the door. Scoot up." After giving him the stink eye, I moved forward and he graced me with a smile. God, he was so yummy. He walked over, stepped in the tub, and lowered down into the water.

Once he settled himself, his arms wrapped around my waist and pulled me back to his hard chest. I snuggled in as close as I could. He grabbed my bath sponge, lathered it up and started washing me. Running the sponge over me, then his other hand over the area to wash it off. I let out a soft moan; it felt so good having his hands over me. He moved and I felt him behind me, pressing against my back. He lowered his head and started trailing his lips along my shoulder, then up my neck. "You're turning me into a machine, Scarlet," he spoke softly.

I turned around and straddled him. I could feel his need to be inside me. I grabbed the sponge from him and ran it over his body, tracing every curve of his chest, shoulders, and arms. He was so defined. My finger traced the scar on his shoulder. I leaned over and pressed my lips to that area. He let out a breath I didn't know he was holding. I continued to kiss him everywhere I could until finally my lips found his. I felt like I needed his lips like a woman in need of water. I tried to pour every ounce of love into this kiss as I could.

He grabbed my hips and pulled me closer, deepening the kiss. I felt so alive. Moans escaping both of our lips as we matched passion with passion. Without words both of us needing the same thing. I lifted up as he guided himself into me. My body convulsed as shivers ran over me. It never ceased to amaze me the feelings he gave me. My eyes fluttered back, his kisses grew with desperation.

I got the hint, I needed to move too. I lifted up and back down, filling myself with him. He guided my hips up, down, up, down. Finding the pace we both needed. Our mouths never left each other as we found our release. It was the most passionate love making I had ever experienced. That's what it was, making love. Did he feel the same way? I wanted to say how I felt, but I just couldn't get the words out. They seemed stuck in my throat. Our kisses slowed down to little pecks. He pulled back and ran his hands along the sides of my face, cradling it. "You are amazing." It felt like he was going to declare something. He kissed me then spoke again. Could this be it? He coughed.

"We should get out of here, don't want to get pruney." Hm, not really what I was secretly crossing my fingers for him to say, but honestly I think I am the only one crazy enough to fall in love this quick. I mean, it's crazy.

CHAPTER 16

DARIEN

Shit, I almost blurted out that I was in love with her. That would have ruined it all, I know she felt something for me, but I seriously doubted she was ready for my declaration of love here. Damn, I was a fool. I let her get up and out of the tub first, then myself. I grabbed the towel and wrapped it around her. Her body was so perfect, it fit me so right too.

"How did your briefing go?" she asked. "Good, I will be spending the next couple days training the next line of Seals, survival teaching. It's one of the things I am one of the best at." She looked at me and nodded.

"So you are like Bear Grylls?" I laughed at her question. Oh Bear Grylls, the ultimate survivor man. We always get compared to him, except we survived actual shit, not just set-up shit.

"I'm better," was all I said. She didn't need to know the details. She looked impressed. Good, I felt ten feet tall impressing her.

After we dried off, I followed and grabbed my trail of clothes strewn about her place. When I got her texts, I needed to get over here stat, and started undressing on the way up. I dressed in my jeans, and she joined me downstairs dressed in a pair of flannel pajama pants and a tight T-shirt. Besides her dressed in nothing but my T-shirt, I think this outfit is one of my favorites. It's so her. There was a symbol on her shirt.

"What does that symbol mean?" I asked. It looked like a triangle with a circle inside and a line drawn through it. She looked down at it.

"Don't worry, young padawan, we will get there." She went over to the TV and put in a DVD. More movie time, fine by me as long as she snuggled that fine ass up against me. She looked back at me. "Wanna hang out and watch a movie with me? I can make us some popcorn."

I walked over and sat on the couch where Roxy was hanging out on. Scarlet beamed at me. Glad I was staying. That was fucking awesome. "What are we watching?" I asked. She smiled and came to sit next to me.

"I figured we could keep going with your Harry Potter lesson." I rolled my eyes, but I actually liked what I had seen so far. I wrapped my arms around her and pulled her close. I kissed her briefly as the movie started.

When the credits started rolling I looked down to see a sleeping Scarlet. She slept like the dead. I wish I could sleep like that. I reached over her and grabbed the remote to turn off the TV. I gently lifted her and cradled her into my arms as I carried her up to her bed. I laid her down and pulled the covers over her. She looked like an angel sleeping.

Until she rolled over and started snoring. I tried to hold back my laughter. She didn't snore any of the other times she had slept with me. A silent laughter slipped through my lips. I started to walk away. I wasn't sure how she would feel if I just lay down with her. A creak in the floorboards made noise and it made her stir. REALLY? I carried her up the stairs and laughed at her and the damn noise of a floorboard made her stir. Damn. She rolled over and saw me. She spoke through her yawn.

"Stay." I walked back over and lay down beside her. She rolled over and snuggled into me again. She found her place at my nook. I smiled. She murmured in a very sleepy voice, "My nook." My chest felt like it was going to explode. "Your nook," I said softly. She could have any part of me she wanted.

I slept with her for a couple hours, and then I woke up, wanting to do a bit of scouting. On the field we took sleep when we could get it, sometimes we wouldn't sleep for days. I hadn't been sleeping well since Summers's passing, but I think I was starting to come back around. No nightmares, or feeling like someone is after me. But someone seemed to be after Scarlet, and that was something I was going to figure out. I will figure it out, I will protect her.

I slowly and quietly untangled myself from her warm, soft body, and walked out of the room. I grabbed my boots by the door, and heard a noise. A whine. Roxy.

Looks like she wanted to go with. She could be useful. After tying up my boots, Roxy and I set off for outside. She sniffed around while I walked the perimeter. No foot prints in the dirt. Good sign. Everything looked intact. No signs of foot traffic.

Suddenly I heard Roxy's strong bark; I took off running towards the dog. She was closer to the main road; a man was on the ground in front of her. I slowed down as I came to her. "Roxy, sit." She sat. Hm, she really was trained well. I'm thankful for that. I turned my attention back to the stranger. He had blond hair, looked like a surfer.

"Who are you and what are you doing here?" I asked with determination in my voice. He looked at the dog, then back at me. "I was just walking, I swear!" Sweat was coming off his face in rivers. His eyes kept dancing between me and the dog. I crouched in front of him.

"Walking this late? Nah... now who are you?"I asked again. "My name is Jimmy. I swear I wasn't doing anything," he answered. "Jimmy, do you know whose house that is?" I pointed to Scarlet's. He nodded.

"Yeah, that is Scarlet Barnette's, she is the self-defense teacher. I volunteer there a lot!" He knew her.

"Have you been sneaking around her house lately? I am a Navy Seal. Just think about all the things I can do to you if you lie to me, so it's not really in your best interest, Jimmy." He nodded, scared shitless. Good.

"I swear. Yes, I have been around. I love to surf and this part of the beach has the best waves. I have been sneaking over to her part of the beach at night sometimes. Really great waves, when the moon is high. I felt bad and stopped by the other day to ask her if it was okay. The door was unlocked so I let myself in thinking she just didn't hear me, but once no one answered I left immediately. I wasn't able to get to her classes this week! I'm so sorry. I swear, man, I won't do it again! Don't hurt me!" He really did look like he was going to piss his pants. I wanted to laugh at this pathetic man.

"Get out of here, and trust me, if you ever come on this property without Scarlet's okay, I will press charges on you for trespassing or do worse." This man was honest enough. I knew he wouldn't be back, not with myself and

Roxy around. He scrambled away and ran like hell from there. I took a deep breath. I felt like I caught the culprit, but the little voice in the back of my head was saying that it wasn't the right one. I guessed we would just have to wait and see.

Roxy and I walked back into the house. I snooped around and found her a treat before heading back to the goddess asleep upstairs. She was definitely a sight after tonight's events. She was safe for now. She rested peacefully, her lips were parted and slightly pouting. I smirked, and went to lie down with her again. A smile came across her lips as I intertwined my hand with hers and fell asleep.

My phone started beeping waking me from my slumber. Shit, where was it? I quietly crawled out of bed and followed the noise down the stairs to the coffee table. My alarm was going off. It was 5:30a.m. I needed to get ready to go to base. I found a piece of paper and pen by the kitchen and wrote Scarlet a note saying I had to go to work, but I would text her later. I went back up the stairs and put the note on the pillow. I grabbed my other clothes and boots and headed over to my house to get dressed.

Fuck, it was cold as the freaking arctic out here. We must be getting a winter storm soon. I quickly dressed in uniform and grabbed a jacket before heading out.

I drove onto base and located LCDR Austin. "Morning, Valentine, are you ready?" He stands at attention and salutes, as do I. "Yes, sir." We relax and head towards the training facility. I see the men the closer we get. Having push-up contests. Good, at least they like getting sweaty.

"Everybody listen up!" LCDR Austin spoke to them. "This is Captain Valentine. He will be training you for the next two weeks." He looked at me, nodded his head, then walked off. Great. I introduced myself to them. They seemed like an eager group of guys.

Over the next few hours we spent time going over some books, did some water treading, had lunch, then after that we did some physical training, and then a five-mile run... fun stuff! I also told everyone it was a requirement to volunteer at Scars at least once a week while I was their instructor. I sent a text to Scarlet after showers.

I think I need another bubble bath after today.

She responds almost immediately. I gotta admit it brings a smile to my face.

Oo, somebody wants to get a rub a dub, dub, in the tub. ;)

My dick was getting hard thinking about last night's rub in the tub. She seems to have a gift of turning me on via text. It's time for me to turn up the heat and make her suffer.

I could go for rubbing my hands over your tantalizing breasts, running my tongue up your pussy, up, down, in, out.

HA! Let her visualize that one! Of course I was totally sporting a hard-on in the locker room now. I have got to get out of here before someone sees it. I finished getting ready then headed out pretty damn quick; it's not that easy to get rid of a hard-on, you know? As soon as I get in the Jeep my phone beeps.

Well played, Valentine, well played.

Damn right well played! I am awesome at everything.

;) So what are you doing tonight?

I'm going shopping with Candace, and hopefully having some hot sex later. You?

Mmm, sex with her is really fucking hot. I don't think it would ever get boring with her.

Going to clean up the house then have some pretty hot sex tonight myself.

See you later then. ;)

;)

My drive to the house passed quickly. I decided for the rest of today I would pack up Aunt Tara's clothes and a few more belongings. I hadn't packed up her things from her dressers or anything because it just felt weird. I packed her clothes away and put them in the attic in case Mom wanted them or something. My stomach started to growl as I was organizing the attic. I decided to go with chicken and a sweet potato. A growing boy like me needs protein. I turned on the TV to watch some hockey while I cooked. Watching sports was something I kind of missed. You don't really get to watch the Super Bowl out on assignments. No sitting on the couch with pizza and wings, just sitting in mud, snow, sand, or in the water.

As the chicken simmered in the pan I thought about that. I love what I do; it felt like I was accomplishing something. It's all I've done since eighteen, but I did enjoy instructing those men today. I liked where things were going with Scarlet too. Of course, either way I would be there for her, long distance or not. I loved the girl. I really wanted to be with her too. I have time to think a little more on it; seven more weeks to figure it out. Dinner was done, thank god, because smelling this delicious chicken made me feel like I was starving. I settled on the couch with my plate and started watching some hockey.

A few hours later, someone knocked on my door. I glanced over to see that beautiful smiling goddess. I walked over and let her in. She tackled me with a hug. "I like the way you say hello," I laughed out. She just smiled and put a hand to the back of my neck and kissed me. A growl came out from my throat as I took her in. Jesus. She consumed me. I pulled us back and closed the door behind her. I wrapped my arms around her, bringing her as close to me as I could. She pulled back and looked up at me with gleaming eyes. She seemed so happy, I loved it. "Hi," she said. I couldn't get the stupid looking grin off my face.

"Hi to you too. You seem happy." She nodded and confirmed she was. "I was just watching hockey, want to join?" I ask. "Sure." She nodded. She put her purse down on the table and joined me on the couch.

As soon as I sat down she attacked me. Kissing me all over, pressing her chest up against me. She found her way into straddling me. I was so fucking ready to have her again. Her hips started moving over me. My mind stuttered to think. Her aggressiveness was mind blowing. She sucked, bit, and licked my bottom lip. FUCK!

My hands travelled to her hips, up her back, everywhere! She still really hadn't said anything significant since she got here, but damnit I needed to be inside her. She paused her assault on me to tear my shirt off over my head. Her mouth crashed back to mine as she continued what she was doing before. Her hands felt greedy as they touched every part of my chest. Another growl came out of my mouth. This was so fucking hot. She ripped open the button dress she was wearing. I hadn't even noticed what she was wearing. Shows you where my mind had been since she got here. I ran my hands over her perfect breasts. I reached around and unclasped the bra and set those babies free. I brought my hands back to her, kneading her. I slightly pinched and she gasped. Our hips were blending together in movement, mine thrusting towards her every move. She continued devouring me, and then moved on to my jaw and neck.

Once she got close to my ear she whispered, "Fuck me, Valentine." Have I fucking died and gone to some sexy heaven? She didn't have to tell me twice! I grabbed her hips and picked her up, her legs wrapped around mine.

"Where do you want it, baby?" She nodded towards the wall. *Hot damn!* Okay! I walked us over towards the wall. We were kissing each other like we couldn't get close enough. I literally ripped her panties off her. She unbuttoned my jeans and slid them down. I grabbed her by the ass and lifted her up and positioned myself between her legs. She pulled me to her. I impaled her in one quick thrust, instantly going at a fast, hard pace. She was screaming her pleasure into me. She was so fucking wet. Her sheath was clenching around me as I pulled out and pushed back in. Relentless. Her nails bit into my shoulders as she clung to me. Her head fell back against the wall, her eyes closed.

"OH DARIEN! GOD! OH...OH!!" I somehow came up with the strength to push harder. Seconds later, she was climaxing around me. Her pussy clenched around me in a death grip, forcing me into my own blissful climax. My whole body convulsed against hers as we came together.

Her head finally came back from the wall and our lips found each other through our heavy breaths. I had to speak up about this sexy assault that just occurred.

"What happened today? I'm quite fond of the mauling that just happened here." She laughed. "Yeah, I was thinking about you a lot today, and then Candace was talking about stuff with Ross, and I was just like...mmm I need Darien." Inner Darien was nodding in approval, patting himself on the back. I couldn't help the chuckle that came through. She shimmied down my body. I knew I had some sort of smug look on my face because she looked at me and shook her head.

"Maybe I shouldn't have made your ego any bigger," she said. I laughed. "It's okay, I know you are addicted. I'm just that good." I winked at her, and she lightly smacked my stomach.

Oh, elementary style flirting, huh? I picked her up and deposited her on the couch to start tickling her. I loved hearing her giggle. "STOP! STOP!" she spoke through her laughter. Taking pity on her I ceased my attack. She composed herself and sat up on the couch. She looked around a little nervously. I kind of was hoping she wasn't going to go after this; when she was with me I slept a lot better. Plus, I liked being with her, the more time the merrier. Gently I lifted my fingers under her chin, lifting her head to look me in the eye.

"I want you to stay with me. Please," I spoke to her softly. "I'd like that," she answered. I pulled her chin close and kissed her with everything I had. After an honest to god make out session, like what you did in high school, she started to yawn. I glanced at the clock and it was about 11:45.

"Why don't you go shower and we'll go to bed."
She yawned again and nodded. "Okay, as long as I get your
nook," she teased. I chuckled and agreed. "My nook is
yours." She smiled, and then got up to go take a shower.

I sat back and took a moment to reflect. Today was
a damn good day. I wanted more days like this. She was
really into me, was it love? I'm not sure. I needed to tell
her how I felt. I know it's crazy since we haven't known
each other long, but I knew right away. I would do
anything for her. Wait. I would do anything for her. That
realization meant a lot. I heard her turn the water off
upstairs and decided it was time to join her in bed.

I walked up the stairs and turned into the bedroom
to see her in one of my T-shirts, snuggling into my bed. A
deep satisfaction rumbled through me. I walked over and
crawled into the bed with her, and moved my hands
across her soft, satin smooth body. She rolled into me and
snuggled in my nook, sighing in contentment.

"Oh yeah, I meant to tell you that friend of yours...
Um, Fox..." I immediately stopped breathing. How dare he

come near her. She continued on. "He volunteered at one of my classes today." My body stiffened at that statement.

"Oh? Did everything go okay?" I didn't want her to freak out. "He kind of gives me the creeps, but he was nice to me. Ross kept an eye on him though." I felt a little relief. Thank Ross man. I was going to have to buy him a six-pack for that. She looked up at me.

"How do you know him?" I didn't really want to answer that question but if he is up to something I felt the need to tell her. "We were in a team together, about four years ago. He was good at translating other languages. He is a really good marksman too. We were sent in to Darfur. A lot of genocide was happening at the time, I'm sure you heard about some of it on the news. There was one camp where some bad guys were holding hostages. We were sent in to take them out. It was easy enough. Something happened while we were taking them and Fox shot almost all of the hostages. He pleaded insanity and was dishonorably discharged. I saw him a few times after. It pretty much comes to blows every time we get around each other. He is nothing but a sinister dick." I held her a little tighter after revealing all of that. I wanted to protect her from any burden. Having that type of knowledge in your head was a burden. She hadn't said anything.

"Don't worry, baby, I won't let anything happen to you." She snuggles in me. "I know," she yawned.

"Night, babe," I whispered into her hair. I felt the smile against me. "Night, Darien." We both fell into a comfortable sleep together.

"I think that's a great idea, baby," I said to Scarlet. After we woke up this morning and had our morning routine of coffee and tea, she told me she was thinking about having a barbeque to celebrate the four-year anniversary of Scars. "I think so too. I will call Candace. She is the go-to person when it comes to party planning," she said as she saunters off to find her phone and call Candace. I thought about my team. I haven't heard from anyone in a while. This would be the perfect opportunity to invite them if they were around. I walked over to the table where my phone was and called Daniels. He was our social butterfly.

He answered on the second ring, "House of we love you long time, how can we service you?" I laughed, he was a trip. "Hey, man, how's it going?" I asked. He knew who I was, it's not like he answers the phone like that with everyone. At least I hoped not.

"Just hanging out waiting on my next assignment. Are you enjoying your leave yet?" he asked. "I really am, man. Actually I wanted to invite you over to a barbeque tonight if you were in town." There was a pause then finally he spoke.

"I think I can make that happen. I'll call the others and see if they can make it. I'm in D.C. right now, but I think we can make it to Norfolk in like three hours. Ericson has been dying to get away." I did miss them. "Sweet deal, just get here whenever. I'll see you then. You know where I live now," I said to him, and then we hung up.

When you have been in the field as much as we have, you kind of make your phone calls short, in case of someone listening in. We did it out of habit, not that anyone would care about a barbeque.

After Scarlet called a bunch of people to invite, we decided to take Roxy for a walk. It was a nice little habit of ours to do, and of course I went all Notebook on her and held her hand and kissed her senseless every chance I got. I figured with the get-together tonight and the trip to the mountains coming up she was practically skipping with joy. I loved seeing her so happy.

As we made our way back to the house there was a red truck in her driveway. I hadn't seen it before and it made me nervous walking with Scarlet towards it. It was covered with New Jersey Devil's stickers. Somehow I didn't think that someone who was here to hurt her would have so much recognizable stuff on their truck.

Suddenly Candace popped out of her front door and walked towards us. "So glad you are back. I got everything set up in the back for later, and I called Tom from Tom's Piggy Party. He is coming over at three to start cooking the pig." She could talk anyone's ears off. I'm glad that Scarlet and I could sit and be comfortable just being quiet together sometimes. Scarlet just beamed when she saw her. I was right, she was ecstatic about this. Therefore, I was too.

Scarlet wrapped her arms around me and gave me a kiss that was full of promise before Candace pulled her off to go work on things for the party. I was thinking about helping when a hand landed on my shoulder. I turned and saw Ross. "Don't do it, man, if you offer to help you won't get out alive. I helped carry tables and I barely got out with my life." He actually looked like he survived the horror.

"Well I do owe you some beer after keeping an eye on Scarlet yesterday. We could sneak over to my house and watch the girls do their thing from the porch." "Now that sounds like a plan!"

We walked over to my house, after grabbing some beers from the fridge we then settled into the rocking chairs on the back porch.

"Do you know that guy who came into Scarlet's class yesterday? Is that what you meant by keeping an eye out for her?" Ross asked.

"Yeah, he was an old team member. He's bad news," I confirmed for him. He just shook his head and looked towards the girls. Candace was going on and on about something while Scarlet was just hanging lights. I looked at Ross. He was completely mesmerized by Candace.

"Dude," I said to him, and he knew exactly what it meant. "Dude," he sighed. It was simply a guy way of admitted he was in deep. I knew the feeling. We sat there and watched the girls do their thing until it was time to party.

The party was in full swing, the food was perfect, the decorations looked awesome, and of course Scarlet was decked out in a nice sweater dress with knee high boots. I was going to have to have some fun with those later. I couldn't think of anything else but taking her back inside the house and having some sexy time. I walked over to where she was chatting with people and wrapped my arms around her. She snuggled into my chest.

Then someone spoke next to me. "I hope you're going to snuggle up to me like that, you big boy." I whipped my head in the direction of the voice. "Ericson! I'll do more than snuggle you." I winked at him. He hadn't changed much. He was wearing a shirt that said "To Women, From God."Still the joker. Next to him was Tanner and Daniels.

Scarlet was now paying attention to the men. I knew what she saw. Ericson was a tall, tanned, blue eyed, blond ladies' man. Tanner had brown hair and blue eyes with big muscles. He worked out a lot. Daniels was looking around, checking out the place. He was tall, with short blond hair and blue eyes, with sideburns and a goatee. They always called us the Blue Eyed Seals. Not very creative, but it worked for us.

I introduced her to each of them. They all hit on her, of course, but knew she was mine and they didn't press any further. We all slapped each other on the backs in hello. Out of the corner of my eye I saw a sharp jaw with a scar. Fox?

I turned towards the person but they weren't there anymore. He better not fucking be here. I looked at my men. They saw the alert in my eyes. I leaned in close to Daniels. "I think Fox is here, scout out the area." He just nodded. He made an announcement to Scarlet.

"Alright, well, I am going to go check out the food and then go take a piss. See you lovebirds around." He winked then took off. Ericson and Tanner drifted off as well.

"They seem nice," Scarlet said. I'm glad she liked them, and they obviously liked her. I always said if my friends didn't like you then there was something wrong with you. After what seemed like forever, the Blue Eyed Seals made their way back to me. They found no signs of Fox anywhere. Could I have imagined it?

After the party was over everyone but Scarlet and I parted ways to their own homes. It was a long day and I needed my Scarlet in boots time. When the last person left I scooped her up and took her upstairs to have my wicked way with her.

The next day went by in a flash. Work. Dinner. Movie. Hot sex. It was a fantastic way for your days to go. Tomorrow would be Valentine's Day, and we would be on the way to the mountains. I was going to put Fox and everything else behind me and just let loose. I decided I was also going to man up and tell Scarlet how I felt tomorrow too. I couldn't wait.

Chapter 17

Scarlet

"I'm so excited! I haven't ever been snowboarding before!" I was squealing as Darien and I set off after having a late lunch for Ross's cabin in West Virginia. I did pretty well by only packing one big snow jacket, two duffle bags of stuff, and my bathroom bag. Darien shook his head as I pulled those bad boys out to my SUV. He only had a medium size duffle and a snowboard and boots to go with it. Little did he know I packed a few of my nerdy costumes in there for him. He admitted he had a dream about me in a Princess Leia costume once. So I figured for Valentine's Day I would surprise him in that costume that I just happened to own once we got there and found alone time. I laughed to myself. It was going to be an awesome Valentine's Day! He wanted to drive. He said something about how I was a woman, and driving on snow. Pish posh to that, asshole! But I decided to let him drive.

I brought my trusty book Obsidian to keep me company if need be. Today had been a really cold day, and we looked on the weather channel earlier to see that it looked like we would get a snow storm once up there. So that would be nice to see some snow falling. As long as it wasn't like a blizzard or anything. I guessed we would just have to see.

"Snowboarding can be fun, but it is a little hard. You might end up switching to skis, but it's okay if you do," he said while switching lanes. We were already into hour three out of a five-and-a-half-hour drive, and we were coming up on 4:30 in the afternoon.

"We are going to have so much fun. Do you know when Ross and Candace left?" I asked. I texted her this morning but she didn't get back to me yet. "Yeah, they left early this morning. I guess they wanted a little alone time in the hot tub before we got there." My nose scrunched up at that. Ew, I was so not getting in that hot tub. Gross.

I was enjoying the change in the scenery, beach to hills and mountains again. There was already some snow dusted on the ground as we passed by. I sometimes missed living in the mountains but definitely not enough to move back. No way in hell. But it was nice to visit. We started making our way up the main mountain. It always made me nervous because the roads were narrow, and, well, there was nothing but a guard rail and then the side of a mountain. It was scary, especially with snow.

Then I suddenly heard my jam! I reached over and turned the volume up. Nervous feeling was gone. I started belting out lyrics. "WHYYYYYY, MY CAR IS IN THE FRONT YARD, AND I'M SLEEPING WITH MY CLOTHES ON, CAME IN THROUGH THE WINDOW LAST NIGHT, AND YOU'RE GONE, GOONNNEEE." I loved this song: My Own Worst Enemy. I looked over at Darien, he was smiling at me. Yeah, I probably looked like a goof, and then he started joining me in singing the lyrics. Which made me smile even bigger. I loved a guy who I could sing and dance around with. It was nice to see a man like him letting loose like that. We were goofing off with all the songs that were coming on the radio after that.

Then, BAM, someone hit the back of my 4Runner. "Oh my god, Darien!" I was scared shitless, I looked back and saw a black Mustang gaining speed towards us. *What the hell was going on?* I looked at Darien. He was very focused on driving, and constantly checking the mirrors. His jaw was locked, he looked dangerous.

He pressed the gas and maneuvered my SUV like it was a sports car going up the zig zags of the mountain. I looked behind us again and the Mustang was about to hit us, when Darien jerked the SUV to the left to avoid it. The Mustang drove up next to us, I tried to get a good look at who was driving but the windows were tinted so dark I couldn't see inside. I was trying not to freak out, but I was super close to having a heart attack. I mean, we were on the side of a mountain for Christ's sake!

The Mustang slammed into us making us hit the rocks on the side of the mountain. I screamed. I was going to die! I did the first thing that came to mind.

"Darien, I'm in love with you!" I screamed out. I didn't want to die and he not know. That would be like some unfinished business for me. He looked at me and cursed. Well that wasn't what I was looking for. I mean, he might not love me back, but cursing after my confession definitely wasn't what I thought would come out of him. His jaw locked up, a little muscle started twitching there.

He turned the car back towards the Mustang. The Mustang pressed the breaks. Thankfully, Darien corrected it, and we didn't go off the side of the mountain. I felt a rush of relief.

Then, BAM, the Mustang hit us in the left taillight making the front of the car go towards the guard rail again, this time the screeching of the metal rail and the car was ringing in my ears. Darien looked in the mirror towards the Mustang and looked me dead in the face. There was pure panic in his eyes. "Scarlet, hold onto something!" he yelled. I grabbed the Oh Shit handle on the ceiling.

I barely had time to grab it when, BAM, the Mustang hit us again and we went through the railing. This was it; my worst fears of going over the mountain were coming true. We rolled over and over. Part of the SUV hit trees, rocks, and just kept going. Like a pinball in a machine. My head hit the window. Glass was shattered and I could feel it going everywhere. I felt a severely sharp pain in my right side; that wasn't good. A warm liquid started coming down my face from my head. I was so going to die. I was losing consciousness when I thought the SUV stopped rolling. I wasn't sure. There was a numbing feeling all over. Everything was quiet, no loud crunching noises of the car, nothing. My eyes closed and I faded into the blackness.

Why was I feeling pain? Dead people don't feel pain. I felt warm, strong arms cradling me. I felt weightless, like I was floating. Was an angel carrying me? I drifted back into the black again.

I felt warm, maybe feverish would be a better word for it. I started to feel a lot now. Before I felt numbness, now I felt aches and sharp pains stabbing at me all over my body. The whole right side of me felt broken. It was painful, but I've had worse.

Christ, there was no way heaven could be this cruel. Somehow I managed to stay alive through the crash.

Darien! Oh no, Darien. Where was he? Was he okay? I slowly opened my eyes. Where was I? I wasn't in the 4Runner. The angel! I must have been carried from the SUV to this, somewhat of a campsite. I tried to call out for Darien, but my voice was very soft. Maybe from screaming so much before? My chest hurt to breathe but I tried again. My voice was laced with panic. Oh god, no one was answering. Please let Darien be around here somewhere, and not some crazy, hermit West Virginian mountain man that rescued me.

"Darien!" I yelled as best as I could again. It felt like my ribs were bruised. Damnit. I tried to get up, a really sharp pain shot through my arm and shoulder. "FUCKING HELL!" I yelled. I looked down and there was a makeshift splint on my right arm all the way up to the shoulder joint. It looked like some of my scarves wrapped around a couple of hard sticks.

A crack of a stick came from the right, my head whipped towards the noise. Please don't be a bear or some dangerous creature. My breathing increased, my heart was pounding so hard I thought it was going to bust through. I tried my best to slowly move away from the noise while keeping my eye on it. It hurt to move, but survival came first. The noise of someone walking came closer and closer until finally a silhouette of a person came into view. The sun was almost gone so there wasn't much light, but I recognized that silhouette.

Darien.

"Scarlet," he said so soft I wasn't sure if he meant it to come out. He dropped the stuff he was carrying and came over to me. Very slowly he came down to his knees in front of me and raised the back of his hand to graze my cheek. Tears sprang free from my eyes as it hit me we survived a horrible accident I was so certain we would die from. I tried to move my arms to hug him but I couldn't get the right one to move. I circled my good arm around him. I sobbed into his chest, as he held me.

After what I would guess would be a half hour, my sobs finally started to cease. He pulled back and cradled my face with his hands as he brought his lips to mine. He kissed me with everything he had. This kiss was like none of the others, so much love, desperation, and need. He broke off the kiss but rested his forehead against mine.

"Scarlet, I was so scared. I thought I was going to lose you." I tried to shush him, to let him know it didn't matter because I was here, but he wouldn't let me.

"No, Scarlet. I could have lost you." He pulled his head back so he could look me straight in the eyes. "I love you, Scarlet. When you yelled it out to me earlier, a piece of me died. I couldn't believe you would love me too, and I was about to lose you after finally having you. You mean everything to me, Scarlet. Everything. You own me completely."

His eyes were dark and very serious. I took a deep breath. My lips seeked his out like a heat-seeking missile. I needed him, like I needed my next breath. I grabbed him everywhere I could with my good hand. He was everything to me. I was so happy we survived the crash, so happy I still had him, and happy we were together.

We kissed until it was necessary to break apart and breathe. I realized I was so focused on how happy I was to be with him, I hadn't gotten a good look at him. I peered back at him, but sadly I could barely see him.

"Are you okay?" I whispered at him, trying to feel my way around his body to see if there was anything broken. "I'm a bit banged up here and there, nothing like your arm and shoulder there. I need to get a fire going. It is going to get real cold tonight." He softly gave me a kiss and then went to work on a fire.

My body was starting to shiver. I didn't realize how cold I was until he mentioned how cold it was going to be. Thankfully by the time my teeth started to chatter Darien got a small fire going. The light from the fire spread about our little campsite. I could finally see his face. He had a cut on his left eyebrow. His left cheek was bruised with a little cut. He shrugged at me and set what looked like a bow made out of shoestring on the ground. I've seen people do that on TV shows. I think they called it a bow drill, where you would twist the wooden drill and use the bow to create friction.

Thank goodness I had him. I didn't think I would be able to do all of this. I took another look around. We were on the ground under a giant rock. Not a cave but like an alcove of some sort. He saw me looking around. "I gathered as much from the wreck as I could." He chuckled a bit.

"Sorry, but I don't know how to tell you this. Your car didn't make it." Asshole... I already figured that one out. "Ass," I barked. I narrowed my eyes at him. I loved that 4Runner. My poor baby.

He continued to speak. "I found your cell phone. Sadly, we don't get cell service on the mountain so it's kind of useless. Couldn't find mine." Well that sucked. You figure you have a phone for emergencies and you can't even use it when you are in an emergency.

"I also found one duffle of yours." His expression grew comical. What was that about? "I'm not sure how useful a Princess Leia costume will be to us, but I'm sure later on I could find some uses for it."

OH MY GOD! He wasn't supposed to see that yet. So embarrassing. "That was your Valentine's Day gift." I rolled my eyes trying to act like I didn't care if he found my secret costume and lingerie stash.

"It is still Valentine's Day, isn't it?" His question was more rhetorical than anything. He walked over into one of the bags and pulled out a bottle of wine. Hm, I didn't pack that. It must be one of his. He grabbed a pillow and one of the big blankets I had packed. I didn't like using other people's pillows. I always brought a pillow and blanket with me when on vacations. Turns out that was a good habit to have. He grabbed a few more things I didn't quite see and came back over to me.

"Here." He wrapped the blanket around me and placed the pillow on the ground on a nice pile of leaves. With the fire going, the area started to heat up a little bit. It kind of felt like we were camping instead of having to do this stuff to survive. He opened the bottle of wine and handed it over to me. I grabbed it with my good hand. "Happy Valentine's Day, Scarlet," he said.

I couldn't express what this meant to me. I felt so emotional with love for him I thought my body was going to explode from feeling so much. It was unreal. "I'd put on my outfit for you, but I think I would freeze. So, another time you'll get your gift." I winked at him and took a swig of the wine. I let out a little whimper. It was so good. I needed a drink after this day.

After a few sips I gave it back to him. The alcohol took a bit of the pain away. I looked at the other things he brought over. I giggled a little. There was my iPod with the ear buds. He found my stash of sour cream and cheddar chips, a little bag of beef jerky, and a bottle of water. Perfect driving snacks and now a perfect Valentine's dinner. "Very romantic," I commented, and he nodded in agreement.

"Well it's not over yet." We ate a little, but tried to save some for later and tomorrow. We talked about what we were going to do. Obviously we wouldn't be going anywhere tonight, but tomorrow Darien was going to climb up the side of the mountain we fell down and try to flag someone down for help. If no cars came by, we were about a thirty-minute drive from a little town, so maybe like an hour walk. I would get to hang out here and wait for him to get help.

After we discussed our plans, Darien grabbed the iPod and helped haul me up to my feet. My body felt unstable standing, and my head starting spinning. He gave me a few minutes to adjust then he placed my feet on his. Just like my dad used to do. I started to tear up. What was he planning? He placed one of the ear buds in my ear and the other in his. He rolled his thumb around trying to find a song. I wondered what he would choose. He started to dance, holding me and moving us both with my feet on his. Music filled my ears and the tears that were hanging back rushed over onto my cheeks. It was Kiss Me by Ed Sheeran. I looked into his eyes through the tears.

"This was my song for you. When I heard it, I thought it was like someone wrote that for me," he said tenderly. More tears ran down my cheeks. He was too perfect.

"I love you, Darien. I thought the same thing when I heard the song. It was so perfect for how I felt. I knew then that I was falling in love with you." He smiled and crushed my body against his more. He kissed me with such passion, such fever. He broke apart and spoke against my lips.

"I knew the moment I met you, you were something to me. I figured it out that first night you claimed my nook that I was falling for you." I pulled back and looked at him. That was only a few days after we met!

"Really? Love at first sight?" He groaned. I gave him a confused look. "Oh god, Scarlet, that night you had me sporting a hard-on and I wanted to go full on caveman over you and take you somewhere and make you scream my name over and over. You were the most beautiful woman I had ever seen. You are my goddess." My heart melted as I became a puddle on the ground. Seriously, I thought guys like him only existed in romance novels like my mom wrote. I crushed my lips to his, telling him everything with my kiss. Pouring all of my feelings into him. He reciprocated the kiss in every way. I pulled back and snuggled into his chest. We listened to the rest of our song together, while he danced for us.

Even though this is a horrible circumstance of being stranded from someone pushing us over the side of a mountain, it has turned into the best day of my life. "Thank you," I whispered. He kissed my head. "Happy Valentine's Day, baby." I sighed from happiness.

We continued to dance through a few songs until I started yawning. We decided we should try and get some sleep. The fire was keeping the area warm and dry, although the ground was still cold, but what can you do? It was hard getting comfortable with my whole right side throbbing, so I snuggled into the blanket against Darien.

"Do you think whoever it was in the Mustang is going to come back for us tonight?" I asked. He shook his head and kissed me on the head. "They probably think we're dead. I'll protect you no matter what anyways. You're mine, Scarlet. I won't let anything take you from me now." I smiled and let the exhaustion take me.

Chapter 18

Darien

Hours passed by and Scarlet started mumbling in her sleep, she was very restless this night. Can't say I blame her, I couldn't sleep. Every time I closed my eyes I saw Scarlet all broken and bloody hanging from the upside-down SUV by the seatbelt. She was like a rag doll when I pulled her out. I gritted my teeth at the thought of losing her, and, shit, I almost had. I had to reset her arm. She had a compound fracture of her radius in her forearm. Thankfully the bone didn't come through the skin, but it had been close. She had to have had some little fractures up her arm, and I think she broke her collarbone because there was a big bump around the joint.

I wanted to punch something. What the hell happened today? Was the Mustang person after her? Or me? She didn't have any enemies, and the one she did was in jail in North Carolina. It made sense if someone was watching saw that I cared for her and the easiest way to get to me would be to get her. I made a lot of enemies over time. But, really? I didn't fucking know and that was pissing me off more than anything. I hated not having all the details. I thought the issue with the person snooping and break in had been resolved when I caught Jimmy, but of course that little voice in my head was right. It wasn't him. I swear if it was that asshole Fox I would kill him. I hadn't heard a peep from him since that night at the club, although he visited Scarlet's job the one time. I sighed, it had to have been him. Why? I didn't know, but I will find him and figure it out if it was him.

I rested my head against the rock wall. Fuck, I couldn't believe this shit. My head was hurting like hell, but I've had worse. I felt so helpless for Scarlet. I knew she was hurting. I remember breaking my wrist when I was a kid and I was doped up on stuff for a few days after to help with the pain. She had no choice. A lot of the luggage from the wreck was scattered about the way down the mountain. I collected as much as I could find, and I was hoping I found her little bathroom bag. I was betting she packed some Advil or something. Although I was intrigued to find her naughty bag, she had costumes and lingerie galore in it. It just reminded me that whenever I found the fucker who ran us off the mountain, and I will, I was going to beat his ass even more for making me miss my vacation of Scarlet wearing those outfits for me. Fucking asshole.

I took some deep breaths and counted to ten. It used to help me when I got into fits of rage when I was in high school. I looked down at Scarlet, her eyebrows were pinched together. I sighed. I wished I could take this all away. Well, not everything. I'm glad we finally got out how we felt out about each other. I was so ecstatic and so pissed when she told me she loved me. I wanted to take her into my arms and kiss her until we needed to breathe, and I was pissed because I thought I was going to lose her. I was waiting for a girl like her to come into my life and be my forever. Not to lose her on a mountain. Thank god I didn't, otherwise no one would be able to stop me from breaking down every damn door in the world to rip that fucker's skin from his muscles, his muscles from his bones.

Suddenly she started thrashing around taking me out of my plans for torture. I grabbed onto her so she didn't hurt herself. "Shhh, baby, it's okay. I'm here." She looked at me and then she bursts into sobs. "Oh Darien." I rubbed her back and cradled her in my arms.

"It's okay, baby. Hey." I slid my fingers under her quivering chin to lift her eyes to mine. Her eyes were red and a little puffy from crying so much, but she was still the most beautiful woman I have ever known. "I love you, we are okay. I won't let anything happen to you." She nodded as more tears slid down her cheeks. She nuzzled into me, and after a few minutes she started to drift off again. My gaze flicked to the fire, it looks like it could use some more wood. Light movement caught my eye to the right. Little fluffs of snow were starting to float their way down. Would it stick? I watched as the blasphemous piece of frozen rain stuck to the ground. Shit. That wasn't going to be good for us. It was already cold as shit out here. We barely had the clothes to stay warm. I couldn't find our snow jackets, otherwise she would be a bit better.

I slowly untangled Scarlet from my body and laid her on the pillow. She seemed to be sleeping better. I walked over to the wood pile I made and added some to the flames. The orange flames licked the wood like little tongues. I crouched down to tend to the flames and think of my plan.

In a few hours, at sunrise, I was going to trek my way back up to the road. Thankfully we didn't go all the way down the mountain. I would say it's about half a mile up, and hopefully I could flag someone down. We would survive this. My fist slammed to the ground. I wanted to scream! I went back over to the most beautiful girl in the world.

I needed to get some sleep before I went up the mountain to get help. I needed to push back everything else and sleep. I lay down on the ground next to her and ran my fingers along her face. Even bruised and cut she was stunning. She reached out for me; I wrapped my arms around her and turned my mind off to sleep.

Soft, feathery strokes across my head woke me. I knew there was no danger now. Those touches I felt down into my soul. There was only one person who could make me feel that way. I was happy to get up. I opened my eyes to see those emeralds staring at me.

"Morning," she spoke softly. I sat up and kissed her. I needed this kiss like it was life or death. She reciprocated the same feelings, her good hand slid across my body. Hello again morning wood. She reached my length and stroked it. I deepened our kiss.

"Baby, I want you so bad. I don't want to hurt you though." I somehow got that out of my mouth. She sighed against my lips. Her warm breath against me was intoxicating, making it very hard to not just take her right here and now.

"I'm sorry, I just couldn't help it. I want you badly." She pulled back to put some distance between us. I got up and looked around. There was about four inches of snow on the ground surrounding us. The fire was still going strong.

"Did you put some wood in the fire?" I asked her. She nodded. Her cheeks had a pleasant flush to them. Not sure if it was from our little heated kiss or from the cold. My long sleeve shirt wasn't doing too much for me but I would survive. I grabbed the bottle of wine we didn't finish and gave her some. She needed to hydrate, and that was all we had left. I needed to get us out of here. I shuffled over to the baggage I found. She didn't have a lot of useful things in her sexy time bag. I found a hat of some sort. It looked like a cat and had long arms coming from it. I held it up. "What is this?" She almost spit out the wine. She coughed for a few minutes after I showed it to her.

"That is called a 'Hatimal.' It's a hat that has kitty ears with attached paws. It's cute." Her chin came forward. I went over and put the hat on her. She reached down and put her bad hand in the paw and then her good hand. She curled her hand like a cat and then the sexiest meow I had ever heard came out of her mouth. I had to laugh about that. She was just too damn cute. I shuffled around more of our things until I came up with the perfect ensemble.

Once I was put together I grabbed a few pieces of beef jerky for breakfast. She was smirking at me. "Hey, don't be jealous. You're just mad because I can pull it off," I said. She was eyeing my outfit. I had to work with what I had and right now I had my long sleeve blue thermal and my red thermal, black with white striped jogging pants over my jeans, a multi colored scarf with matching hat. Yeah I probably look a little off, but that was beside the point. She laughed.

"Yes you wear accessories quite well." I winked at her. The sun was starting to come up. It was time for me to go. I walked over to her and crouched down. I reached out and touched her. She just nodded. I wouldn't say goodbye to her because there was no way in hell I wouldn't see her again. "I love you. You are my forever, Scarlet. I'll be back." I kissed her quickly but passionately. I couldn't linger, otherwise I would never leave. When I pulled back she spoke with determination.

"I love you, Darien. I'll see you in a bit." I tucked the blanket around her more and added more wood. She needed to stay warm while she waited.

I grabbed my M9 out of my bag and stuck it in the back of my jeans. I turned towards her again before I left. She just smiled at me and waved bye. I took off towards the road. I passed the SUV a few minutes later. It started getting steep after that. Damn, I was glad I always wore boots. A few times I had to use my hands to climb up, and damn if that wasn't cold. I was starting to sweat being bundled in all these clothes, as I continued to make my way up the mountain. I saw debris from her car as I climbed up. Part of her bumper was attached to a big pine tree. It must have hit it when we were playing pinball with nature.

About thirty more minutes of climbing, I was starting to see a clearing up ahead. I dug the balls of my feet harder and pushed on. I was so close. Finally, I reached where we were pushed through the guard rail. It looked horrible. As I finally made it to the pavement someone yelled out. "Sir! Sir! Are you okay?" I was never happier to see a police officer in my life. I couldn't help the triumphant grin that made its way onto my face. He talked into his radio about how he found a survivor.

Once he reached me, he flooded me with questions about the accident. Apparently he was heading up the mountain and saw the broken guard rail and made a call. An ambulance was on their way, firefighters, and the works. I told him about Scarlet, and he ordered a helicopter to come and get her, since there was no way someone was going down the mountain and dragging her up. It took a lot out of me just to do it by myself. I was so happy we made it.

An hour later I was on my way with the officer that found me to the hospital they were taking Scarlet to. The EMTs on the helicopter said she did have a broken collarbone, along with a few stress fractures in her humerus. The compound fracture I set back for her, and they think she bruised a few ribs too. But she will have to get x-rays and cat scans when she got to the hospital. I hated waiting to see her. It was about an hour drive down the mountain to the hospital she was at. I told my story to the police offer. He was going to put out a report for a black Mustang with some damage. See if anyone saw the car.

As we pulled into the hospital parking lot, I took off and ran to find my girl. I passed by a reception desk. "Excuse me, can you tell me where Scarlet Barnette is? She was just flown in." She took her sweet time looking me over. Okay, lady, you can ogle me as I leave to find Scarlet.

"Sure thing, doll." My patience was thinning as she very slowly licked her lips and walked over to the computer to figure it out. She turned towards me. I was practically staring at her with all of my attention. "She just got done with the x-rays. she is in room two twenty-one. Are you a relative?" she asked.

"Nope, she's my girlfriend," I blurted out and walked off towards the elevator. The elevator was taking forever and I was stuck listening to crappy music while I waited. Finally, the door dinged open and I took off. I came to her door and took a breath.

A nurse was going on about her temporary splint. She was going to have to get a hard cast in about a week once the swelling went down. As soon as the nurse left I let myself in. Scarlet was just looking off towards the window, she hadn't noticed I was there yet. She took my breath away. I couldn't move. I felt like my knees were going to give out. I was so glad we made it. She must have sensed me. Her head whipped towards me and the biggest smile appeared on her face. "I was wondering when you were going to get here. I mean, you don't half-ass a rescue do you? A helicopter? Really?" She was teasing me. I would have called the damn armed forces if I needed to. She is just that important. I just smirked at her and shrugged.

I walked over to her and sat down on the bed touching her anywhere I could. "How are you?" I breathed out.

"I have a compound fracture of my radius, which I'm sure you knew because they said you must have set it." I nodded. That hurt me just as much as it probably hurt for her when I had to do it. It was horrible, I would never forget it. She continued, even though I'm sure I had a face of sadness.

"I have some stress fractures in my humerus, my collarbone was broken but not completely which was nice. I have a few bruised ribs and I am having vertigo pretty badly. They want to keep me here tonight just to make sure I don't have a concussion." Her little cuts here and there were cleaned up as well. Thankfully it looked like she didn't need to get any stitches anywhere.

"So are you all doped up so you won't feel anything?" I asked, trying to lighten the mood. She laughed. "Yeah, they just gave me some. I usually just sleep when on pain pills, so I will probably be in and out of sleep while they watch me for a concussion." I kept smirking at her. I bent down and kissed her as soon as she finished talking. She whimpered, and a growl came out of my throat. She tasted sweet, like the wine she must have finished off.

A cough interrupted our moment. I looked towards the door. The nurse was just coming in to look at something. I turned back to Scarlet who was blushing pretty hard. "Um, Nadine, this is Darien." She paused, like she didn't know how to introduce me. I guess we hadn't talked about it but we definitely were something.

"Her boyfriend," I added. Scarlet beamed at me again. Nadine came over and shook my hand. She asked Scarlet a couple of questions, made some notes on her chart, and exited the room.

"So we are official now?" she asked shyly. "Yep, you are mine." I shrugged as if it was just a fact.

"You can make it Facebook official now if you'd like." I winked. She tried to smack me with her good arm. It was cute.

"So, I guess I am going to be hanging out in here with you. I think I am going to use your little bathroom over there and clean up. Do you need me to do anything for you?" She pondered for a minute. "Actually I am starting to feel a little drowsy from the medicine, do you think you could call my insurance company so we can report my car and get a rental, and, oh! Call Ross so they know about everything!"

"Sure thing, babe. I'll be your secretary. Want me to do anything else?" I wiggled my eyebrows at her like I was trying to insinuate something dirty. She just shook her head, like I was crazy. "I love you," I said. She snuggled into the hospital bed. "I love you too, baby." I liked it when she called me baby. I turned and went into the bathroom to try to become human Darien again instead of mountain man Darien.

CHAPTER 19

SCARLET

I wasn't sure how much time had passed, I was still feeling drowsy. Medicines like this and I never really got along. They made me so tired, but at least there wasn't any pain. I tried to sit up, but there was a steel band of an arm wrapped around me. I looked up into Darien's sleeping face. His lips were parted. He looked so handsome, and he was all mine.

It seemed kind of weird calling him my boyfriend considering everything. He was just so much more for me. He had done so much for me. He became my everything. I hoped that now we made it through this that nothing else would happen. I mean, surely the person that ran us off the mountain thought we were dead. I thought back to when I was sitting in the campsite waiting for Darien. I kept going over the scene in my head. I tried to think of anyone I knew who could do such a thing. I thought of Frank immediately but he was in jail in Asheville so that was impossible. Then there was Darien's old team member, Fox. He gave me the creeps. He was 6', and had a short buzz cut hairstyle. His eyes looked like he was trying to see through my clothing the first time we met. And at my class he looked like he wanted to eat me. I got goose bumps thinking about it. I knew there was bad blood between him and Darien, but enough that he would do something like this? I don't know. I could see it. He seemed like an evil man. I shivered, which woke Darien. "Are you okay, baby?" He panicked. I looked at him and nodded.

"You look so tired. Go back to sleep, baby," I told him. He probably didn't get too much sleep yesterday. I knew he would be worried about me, and was trying to keep an eye on everything to make sure we were okay. He was a leader, a caretaker, but he needed a break. I kissed his cheek.

"Go back to sleep. I'll be right here in my nook." I snuggled into his nook as I spoke. He kissed my head and fell back asleep quickly. I felt the drugs take me to sleep again as I focused on his breathing.

I woke up to the sun shining in through the window. I moved my good hand over my eyes trying to block away the light. Ugh I wasn't ready to wake up. I was dreaming about a bath tub and Darien. Yeah, it was a good dream. Darien? The pillow I was on smelled like him, but he wasn't there.

"Darien," I croaked out. My voice sounded awful. I found a glass of water next to the bed and took a sip. The water felt so good going to my desert of a throat. Darien walked through the door a few minutes later.

"Hey, there's my girl! How are you feeling?" He sauntered over and sat next to me. He touched my face, grazing his hands across my cheek. I loved it when he did that. Tingles ran straight through my body. He consumed all of my thoughts.

"Scarlet? Are you okay?" he asked again, and I realized I hadn't said anything to him. His touch completely made my mind go blank. I tried to focus. I cleared my throat before talking. "Sorry, um, I'm feeling fine. The medicine is starting to wear off, but I think I would be okay with just an Advil. How about you?" He shrugged.

"I'm good. I took care of all those phone calls you wanted me to make. The car insurance dropped off a car this morning. Candace was frantic and is going to meet you at home. She is determined to be your nurse when you get back." I just rolled my eyes. She was never going to leave me alone. "Great," I said with sarcastic enthusiasm. "I'll be there with you. You won't be alone to face the little pixie." I had to laugh at that! She was such a pixie.

"Are they going to let me go soon?" He nodded. "Yep, just go sign some papers whenever you are ready and we are free to go." He was smiling. God, he had an amazing smile. A mouth full of pretty white teeth. I would have to thank his mama for that. I pulled the blanket off and swung my legs to the opposite side. As I got up the vertigo hit, the room was spinning again. I took deep breaths until it went away. He walked around the bed and held onto me to help steady me. His face was full of concern. "I'm okay, it just takes a minute to go away." I pulled away and walked over to grab my dirty crash clothes.

I really wanted a shower and some fresh clothes. As if reading my mind Darien spoke. "Sorry, I couldn't go get us some new clothes." I shook my head. I didn't want him feeling bad about it. I was tough. I was just about to go to the bathroom to change out of the hospital gown when Nadine knocked on the door.

"Hey, guys, I know you have a long trip back. We wanted to give you these, so you wouldn't have to ride all the way back in your accident clothes." She handed us a pair of scrubs. Bless her heart. I was so thankful for everything they had done, but this was just, well, there were just no words. I could feel tears building up. "Thank you," Darien and I said in unison.

I quickly rushed to the bathroom so no one would see my glistening eyes. I tried to put my clothes on but I was just too sore to do it. "Darien?" I called out. He opened the door a smidge. "What's up?" I chuckled. I wasn't used to asking for help so it was kind of a struggle, the words seemed stuck. He stuck his head through the door to see me when I didn't answer. His eyebrows pinched together. "Here, let me help you." I could just hug him. He just knew it was what I needed. Slowly he helped me get into my clothing, every touch made my blood feel on fire. It was so hard not to jump his bones in the bathroom. My breaths started picking up when his hands ran over my breasts and waist as he pulled down the top. He sucked in a breath.

Our eyes met, and like a spark we attacked each other, mouths colliding, tongues meshing. Completely consuming. It was so much. My body was screaming, both for him and because of the pain. I felt him hard against my stomach. I groaned. I wasn't sure how we did it but we managed to get even closer to each other. His hands ravished me. I sucked in a sharp breath as his hand ran over my ribs, and, damn, it hurt like hell! He pulled back. He immediately took his hands off me.

"I'm sorry, Scarlet." The pain was still there. I closed my eyes and took a deep breath. It hurt to breath but after that it was okay. "It's okay, I'll be fine." He looked like he was in agony, knowing he put me in even a little pain. I didn't like that look. I raised my good hand to his face.

"It's okay, Darien, I'm fine. It's just a little sore." He sighed. "I am just going to keep my hands off of you until you heal up." My face scrunched up.

"I'm not sure that's going to work." He just shook his head. I guess I would have to make him change his mind, but not here in the bathroom. "Okay." I grabbed his hand. "Let's go home," I told him, as I led us out into the room. It took no time at all to sign my discharge papers and make our way home.

Finally, after that long ride, we finally made it home. I was so relieved to be back in the comfort of my own home. Darien got out and walked around to help me get out of the car. He was so good at taking care of me. Aunt Tara had been right, he was a jack of all trades. He was a god in bed, a nurse, a good dancer, and Bear Grylls. I was one lucky lady he wanted to be with me. I smiled to myself at that thought. He was mine. My Valentine. I chuckled at that.

His right eyebrow raised in curiosity. Nope, I wasn't going to tell him that he finally broke my Valentine's Day curse, and his name was Valentine. It was destiny, I guess.

He walked to the trunk and pulled out two bags. One is his, and the other is my bag of lingerie goodies. I blushed. I didn't know the EMTs grabbed that. Darien smirked.

"I couldn't let them forget to grab these. I don't think I could go on if I wouldn't be able to ever see you in that Princess Leia costume." I laughed a real, true, deep down laugh. We were home, and alive. It was a time for celebration.

A loud shriek came from my house. I looked towards the noise to see a frantic Candace running towards me. It looked like she was going to crash into me, and she did. I yelped as she squeezed me. Then her mouth started moving a mile a second.

"OH MY GOD! Scarlet, I'm so sorry, oh my god, I missed you. I was so worried, and we didn't know what happened to you! I was freaking out! Are you okay? How are you feeling? Do you need anything? Oh I'm so happy to see you!" She hugged me again but lighter. It was good to see her again, although she was going to be the overdramatic mother to me. Her hug lasted like five minutes.

After she released me she was sporting tears down her cheeks. "Oh Candace, I'm so happy to see you," I told her. More tears rolled down her face. Her eyes turned towards Darien. She mouthed thank you to him. Ross came out and gave Darien a big bear hug. My chest grew with happiness seeing everyone together. Candace grabbed my hand and led me inside. Roxy came barreling towards me. She was happy to see me too. I bent down and gave her kisses and petted her. I walked over to the cabinet and gave her a treat, which she accepted happily.

We all sat down in the living room and talked about what all happened. Candace's face was full of emotion, from panic to tears of joy. Ross looked concerned throughout the story. He kept asking Darien if he knew who did it. We still didn't know for sure, but I'm sure Darien would find out. We ordered takeout, and just relaxed together. I snuggled into Darien as we just chatted on about random things. Having everyone together, my best friend and his together, everything was perfect.

I needed to find out more about her and Ross later. They were looking pretty serious, glued to each other. I was so happy for her. Darien kissed my head, his fingers were rubbing my arm as he held me. I was glad he was okay with touching me like this at least. I would pin him to the ground if I had to.

I was going to have to call Bethany, my occasional substitute for Scars. Of course I wouldn't be able to do anything at work until I healed. The clock started to round 10:30 when I started yawning. "Let's get you to bed, babe," Darien whispered to me. I nodded. I was tired. Darien scooped me up into his arms as he stood up. We said our goodbyes, and he carried me upstairs, which was definitely unnecessary, but I was in no condition to stop him. He set me on the counter in the bathroom and started the water in the tub. Thank god! As tired as I was, I was not going to sleep all nasty. He even put bubble bath in it. Ah, he was perfect!

He slowly and carefully undressed me, and helped me into the tub. The warm water felt heavenly, it made all of my sore muscles feel like mush. I wish I could get my right arm wet, but it was in the temporary cast, so no water for it. A few cuts I didn't know I had stung a lot.

Darien climbed in behind me and started to wash us. After our soak he lifted me out of the tub and dried me off. I walked over and crawled into my comfy bed. Darien climbed down next to me and pulled me against his bare chest. His hard, muscular arms surrounded me. I hummed with delight. He kissed my head.

"I'm so happy we are back here," he whispered into my hair. "Me too, thank you for everything, Darien." He kissed my head again. "Anything for you. Good night, babe." I brought his hand to my lips. "Night."

Four weeks passed almost in the same manner. Darien took care of me, well, Candace ended up coming over every day and taking away most of his duties while she mothered me. We watched TV, movies, played games, he ended up having to go back to the base and train people. I got my permanent cast on a week after we got back. I went with blue and of course everyone signed it.

You're my bitch! Love ya! Candace

Candace is my bitch so I guess that makes you my bitch too! ;) Ross

FUCK THAT! You are only my bitch. Can't wait till this comes off!;) LOVE, your boyfriend who is dying to meet Princess Leia, Darien

Even Darien's family came to visit. They showered me with hugs and food. Darien and I were happy as hell. Candace, Ross, Darien, and I all wanted to go out to dinner. Candace helped me into a nice dress with a sweater jacket to go with it. She even did my makeup and hair since it was hard to do it with one hand.

She finished the final touches on my eyes when she said. "There. B-E-A-UTIFUL!" I looked in the mirror. She did a soft purple eye shadow with a little splash of gold to accent my eyes. The few cuts I had on my face had healed and thankfully no scars formed. I had a scab on my head from hitting the glass, but my hair covered it. She pulled my hair up into a messy bun with little ringlets falling down. It was nice to be able to dress up.

I turned around and looked at Candace, she was smiling at me. "Thank you, I love it! You look gorgeous too. Ross won't be able to contain himself." She blushed.

"He told me he loved me last night." My mouth dropped open. I was so happy for her!

"Oh my god! That it so amazing! What did you say? Do you love him?" I asked. She sat down on my bed.

"I love him so much. I wouldn't think it possible. But I do." I just sat next to her and put my good arm around her, and leaned my head against hers.

"I know the feeling, babe." She just nodded. "Darien really loves you. He would do anything in the world for you. I'm so happy you found someone, babe. Especially after everything you 'vet been through." I didn't want to start tearing up, so I gave her a big fat kiss on the cheek and got up.

"Alright, bitch, let's go get our men. Lord knows what they are getting into." We laughed together at the thought and rushed downstairs.

Dinner was fantastic! It was a comedy lounge, so we got entertainment and dinner! We laughed so hard I thought I was going to piss my dress, which would have been embarrassing. Darien needed to stop at the gas station to fill up the Jeep before we headed home. Sadly, I hadn't gotten a new car yet, so I had to be chauffeured if I need to go somewhere. I told Ross and Candace they could go on ahead of us to my house. We were going to share a bottle of wine I had stashed away somewhere. Darien made an announcement he had some big news to tell us, but he was going to wait until we were at the house. Excitement was building inside of me. I had no clue what Darien was going to say. I was hoping he was going to tell me he was staying to be an instructor, and not going back into the Seals. But that was selfish of me. Of course I would be with him no matter what he chose, but I did like having him around.

"What are you thinking?" he asked as he got back in the Jeep. "I was just thinking about how excited I am about hearing your big news." He grinned and pretended to zip his lips and throw away the key. Really? I just shook my head at his childish act.

We pulled into the driveway and I saw lights on at the house. I was so hoping Candace and Ross weren't christening my couch. Yuck. "Hey, I gotta go run over to my house and get something, I'll meet you over in like five minutes." I nodded. Wondering what he was up to. AHH, I was so full of suspense I thought I was going to burst! "Okay, see you in a few." I leaned over and gave him a kiss. It was a little more intense than what I was going for but what the heck, we hadn't had sex since the accident because my ribs were still tender, but they were better now. Hopefully tonight was the night! Otherwise I might turn into one of those alley cats who walk around with their tails up and meowing every time he comes near me. That would be sad. He pulled back. "See you in a few." He winked and strolled over to my side to open the door and help me out.

I strolled up the stairs and let myself in my house. "Candace, I'm here," I called out. It was very quiet in the house. They must be lip locked somewhere. I put my purse on the counter and walked towards the bathroom. Something caught my eye to the right. There was a spilled glass of wine on my tan carpet. Assholes.

"Candace, you bitch, you spilled wine on my carpet!" I walked over to the glass and saw Candace and Ross lying on the ground. Motionless. *OH MY GOD.* I fell to the ground and crawled towards them. I shook Candace trying to wake her up.   A chill went down my spine. I felt for a pulse, *THANK CHRIST!* She had one. I saw Roxy lying on the other side of Ross. She had burn marks on her side but I could tell she was breathing. What the hell was happening?

"Hello, Scarlet." I froze. My mind, everything just stopped. I think even time stopped. No! It was impossible! I slowly turned towards that horrible voice.

"It's impossible," I whispered. Frank stepped out of the shadows of the hall. He was standing there looking down at me. His eye twitched, his lips grew into the most evil grin I had ever seen. Oh god.

"Actually, Scarlet, it is quite possible. They let me go for good behavior, since I am a born again Christian and all." He did bunny ears with his fingers on the born again Christian part. I was completely frozen to the floor.

"What do you want?" He slowly walked towards me, cold shivers ran through my body. His smile was sinister. He had a plan, and it definitely wouldn't be good for me. He crouched in front of me and tried to touch my face. I smacked his hand away. His eyes turned to a dangerous hunger. I didn't like that face. He wanted me, and he would try to take me whether I wanted it or not.

The alarms in my head were screaming DANGER, DANGER! He cocked his hand back to hit me in the face. As soon as he let it fly I blocked it with my left arm and kicked my feet out to take him off balance. I was stronger than I was before. I knew more. Tears started escaping to my cheeks as I remembered everything he had ever done to me, and to add to all of that he pushed us off that damn mountain. He grunted and came back at me. He took a swing at me and missed, then came back with a jab to my side, which he hit, and it hurt. I head-butted him and he stumbled back a few feet. He was turning more dangerous by the minute. He ran at me, I kicked him but it did nothing. He smashed into me knocking me down. I let out a scream. He immediately started punching me. He got a few good ones on my face I knew wouldn't be pretty. I felt my lips split open.

I needed to get out of this quick.

I took my knee and rolled it to the side which meant he either went with my knee or I break his ankle.

He went, and tried to punch again, but I blocked it with my cast. The vibrations hurt from it, but, fuck it, I would break my arm again if it helped. With that idea I smashed my cast into him. He fell back against my end table and smashed the lamp that was sitting there. He yelled out from the pain.

I scrambled away from him, desperately trying to get away. He rose up and came after me. He stood about six feet away from me when he pulled out a gun from the back of his pants. Oh shit. I wouldn't be able to dodge a bullet. I thought of Darien. I hope he was safe from this.

Frank started yelling "YOU WHORE, I WAITED FOR YOU. YOU ARE MINE! YOU WILL BE MINE OR NO ONE ELSE'S! DO YOU WANT ME TO KILL YOUR BOY TOY? I WILL SLIT HIS THROAT AND LET YOU WATCH HIM DIE BEFORE I KILL YOU." Then Darien kicked down the door. A sense of dread and hope filled me. I didn't want him in this, he could get hurt, but he might be able to save both of our asses.

CHAPTER 20

DARIEN

MINUTES EARLIER

Got it! I looked down an Aunt Tara's wedding ring. She left it in the nightstand with a note addressed to me. I found it about two weeks ago. I couldn't think of a better way to end my leave. I looked at the note one more time before I should go.

Darien,

I wanted you to have this. You are the most amazing man I have ever known. You deserve every happiness in the world. I hope you find a girl that is just as amazing as you. Your uncle gave this to me after only knowing me for a week. It was his mother's. He said it was good luck because they were together for sixty-five years before they passed. He swore the moment he met me, he knew I was the one. I didn't think it was possible, but he showed me it was. One quote I will always remember from a movie Scarlet and I watch, which, by the way, I hope you meet her soon, "A life without love is no life at all." You need love, Darien. Life as a sailors an honorable life. But love will give you a life beyond thought.

I love you,

Aunt Tara (the biggest bad-ass aunt ever!)

I needed a life with love, with Scarlet. I put the note away and the ring in my pocket. I strolled, well, more like ran, my way downstairs. I left the house and started towards Scarlet's. I was so excited to tell them that I had accepted the position of training survival and combat for new Seal teams. I wanted them to learn what saved my life and Scarlet's on the mountain.

Plus, I would get to be with her. What could be better? I was so distracted by the thought of Scarlet in a white dress sauntering down an isle towards me, then her round belly with our kid, I didn't notice the silhouette of a person sitting on her stairs.

"Such a big smile, Valentine, are you that happy to see me?" I stopped.

Fox.

Son of a bitch

"What the fuck are you doing here?" I spat out. Just the sight of him made my vision red, he just shrugged. "Working." My pissed off level was starting to boil.

"You better not have harmed Scarlet, or I swear, Fox, I will kill you." He tsked, and waggled his finger at me.

"You see, Valentine, I am not the one after her. I'm just the hired hand." I gave him the glare of death.

"What the hell are you playing at, Fox?" He smiled and showed all of his teeth, and winked.

"I think you know. Who is the one person who would want to see our sexy Scarlet?" Frank. Shit, I ruled him out because he was in jail. Damn it all to hell. He must have gotten out without her knowing. I should have checked up on him.

"You were always a smart man, Valentine. I knew you would figure it out. He found out about my services, if you will, when he was in prison. He sought me out and hired me. I was the distraction. Keep an eye on Scarlet, figure out her life, freak her out with the break in. You know, make her lose her sense of security. Gotta say though, I didn't mind keeping an eye on her. She is one fine piece of ass, especially in whatever the hell you call those scraps of clothing she wears on the beach. You know the ones she does yoga in." I knew it was him that broke into her house. Something inside me just fucking knew it!

"You pushed us off that fucking mountain!" I spat. He just laughed. "Nah, I didn't get to have the honor of doing that. That was all the crazy man himself."

That pissed off level I mentioned earlier, yeah, that fucker had been blown to bits. I was going to lay this fucker out and go save my girl. He was baiting me, I knew it. He wanted me to lose control. Most men made mistakes when they got angry. Me? It just made me more determined. He continued on.

"I wasn't expecting you to enter in the picture, funny how that happens." I heard a scream come from the house. My insides turned cold. I stopped breathing. He made a low whistle.

"I guess the party has already gotten started. Guess I should get on with mine too." He wasn't going to stop me from getting to her. "I'm giving you one last chance. Fox.

Get the hell out of my way." He stood. "Not going to happen, a asshole." He spit in my direction.

He came at me, swinging first. I moved to the right dodging his fist. I punched his side as his arm passed me. A grunt came from his mouth. His elbow smacked me right in the cheek as he brought his arm back to a neutral position. We switched taking blows to the face until he tackled me to the ground. The ground was my area. He was going to be finished.

He had me in a full mount and was trying to get a punch onto my face, hoping to knock me out. He cocked his right hand back to throw the killer punch. At the same time he started to swing I lifted my hips in the direction he was going which threw him over my head. I scrambled around and caught him in an arm bar as he went to strike me. I didn't even hesitate snapping his arm. He yelled out as I heard the distinct crack of his arm.

His eyes filled with pure hate as he dislocated his shoulder and brought his body over to kick me off of him. He was fucking crazy, but I wasn't done. He was getting frantic. He came at me full speed and swung with his good arm. I caught him by the arm and interlaced my arms under his and around his head. I heard commotion in the house and didn't wait a second before I twisted my hands and CRACK! Fox went limp in my arms.

I lowered his body down and took off for the house. I heard a man yelling. "YOU WHORE, I WAITED FOR YOU, YOU ARE MINE! YOU WILL BE MINE OR NO ONE ELSE'S! DO YOU WANT ME TO KILL YOUR BOY TOY? I WILL SLIT HIS THROAT AND LET YOU WATCH HIM DIE BEFORE I KILL YOU." I kicked down the door and saw the scene.

A tall, tanned man with long black hair that was tied back behind his head was holding a gun at a scared to death Scarlet. I looked her over. She had mascara tear stains down her face. Her lips were split, and her cheek was a little red. *I'LL FUCKING KILL HIM!* There was such fear in her eyes.

"You must be the man she is whoring around with?" He cursed out. I didn't take too well with him calling her a whore.

"She just threw that pussy at anyone, huh?" He looked at her again, as he pointed the gun at me.

"Don't worry, whore, I will fuck away the memory of all these men who you let fuck you." I ran and tackled the man. I heard a shot go off but had no clue where it went. He was strong. He must have worked out a lot while in jail but he was no match for me. I swung at him until I felt he stopped resisting. Blood spattered my hands and clothing.

"Darien, stop, he is out! Darien!" I heard Scarlet scream. It took everything in me to just get off him and go to her.

I fell to the ground in front of her and scooped her into my arms. She sobbed away into my neck. Her hands grasping onto my torn shirt from my fight with Fox. I pulled back to get a look at her.

"Are you okay?" I asked. Her face was starting to swell more and turn a shade of light purple. I noticed her cast looked smashed. She noticed me seeing it.

"I'm okay, he got me a few times, but I got him too. I think I broke my arm again but it was worth all of the pain to hit that jackass." I let out a startled laugh. She fought him, I knew she would. "How is your arm?" My eyebrows came together in confusion.

"My arm?" I looked at both my arms and, *HOLY SHIT*! My left arm was bleeding. That fucker shot me! It grazed the side of my deltoid. I hadn't even felt it. Must be all the adrenaline. Although now that I saw it, I was starting to feel it. Damnit. She started to smile when she figured I didn't even know I had been shot.

I loved her so much. I couldn't wait any longer to tell her everything.

"Scarlet, will you marry me? You are everything to me. I will love you all of my life. I know we haven't known each other too long, but I've known you were my forever all along." I just blurted out. She started crying. Good? Bad? I couldn't tell. She tackled me like a lioness to her prey. She started raining kisses over me.

"Yes! I love you so much, Darien." I hugged her tightly against me, never going to let her go. I fished the ring out of my pocket, grabbed her left hand, and slide it on her finger. She saw it and more tears busted from her eyes.

"Aunt Tara's ring. I always thought it was so beautiful. I love you, Darien." We were so happy.

"Too bad you'll never get to see that day."A bitter voice spat out. I turned towards Frank. He was barely able to hold the gun, but he somehow found the strength. Blood was running from his head and lips. I saw the intent in his face just as he pulled the trigger. I pushed Scarlet to the ground and covered her body with my own. I felt a sharp pain in my chest. I quickly looked at Frank, he was lying on the ground with blood flowing out of his mouth. He was dead. Scarlet was safe.

"Oh no, Darien! No, no, no, no, Darien!" Scarlet was crying out. I looked down and saw where the pain in my chest was coming from. I got shot. I fell back. She scrambled over and put pressure on the wound, with tears streaming down her face.

"Darien, it's going to be okay," she kept saying.

"Oh my god, Scar!" Candace? I didn't know what happened to them, they must just be coming to or something.

"Call 911 now!" Scarlet yelled. My vision was starting to get a little blurry. "I love you," I got out.

"I love you, Darien. You are not going to die on me now. We still have to get married. I'm going to be Mrs. Valentine. Darien. I won't survive this, you have to fight, baby, fight!" she spoke through her sobs. She was being so strong. I loved hearing her say Mrs. Valentine. "Scarlet, move over! I'll handle this." Ross, my man. My eyes closed and I drifted off.

Chapter 21

Epilogue

One Year Later*

Scarlet

"No, No, NO! I can't do this!" I screamed. I had never ever felt pain like this in my life! It was horrible! I don't think I will be able to survive this!

"I can't do this anymore! AHHHH!!!" I cried out.

"Baby, you have no choice now, you have to. We did natural this far, now we can't get an epidural. You can do this, baby, we are almost there!" My husband spoke calmingly to me. Of course he could. Him getting shot in the chest was nothing compared to pushing a giant watermelon out of your vagina!

"HOLY HELL!" I groaned again. He tried to soothe me, but it wasn't helping. "Baby, think happy thoughts. Remember what the doctor said, you need to stay calm."

Screw him! Screw the doctor! I just need to get this little demon out of my body!

I tried to think happy thoughts. I thought about how happy I was when Darien came to after they did surgery to save him when Frank shot him. I was so scared. But he made it. I thought about our wedding day. It was magical. We got married in our back yard on the beach in April. We decided to keep my house, and give his house to Candace and Ross as an early wedding present. We had flowers of all colors strewed about the sand. It was a small wedding, just family and close friends. Even my parents made it, I was so happy. My strapless dress trailed lightly behind me as I walked down the aisle towards him. He was a stunner in a buttoned-down cream shirt, and khaki pants. We said our I dos and danced to our song under the lanterns and stars on the grass.

About a month later we found out we were pregnant. Darien was ecstatic. He had been the best partner in life any one could ask for. He was perfect. He even rubbed my feet and did 3:00 a.m. milkshake runs for me. Thinking about our wedding was helping with the contractions, until the baby started crowning.

"OHHHHH MYYYYYY GOOOOOOOOOOOODDDDD!!!!!!!!!!!!!!!!!!" I screamed at the top of my lungs. Then there was nothing. Just relief. A baby's cries erupted into the room. Tears started running down my face.

He was here. Our little angel. I couldn't believe it. I was a mother. Darien kissed me as we watched the doctor place our son on my chest. He was beautiful. I looked at Darien, his eyes were full of tears. It was just as beautiful seeing him so emotional over seeing our son. "I love you, baby, thank you," I said to him. He kissed me again. "I love you, baby. Happy Valentine's Day." I laughed. My favorite holiday.

Letter to the Reader

Dear fabulous reader,

Thank you, thank you for taking the time to read this book. I hope you were giddy with enjoyment reading it as I was writing it.

If you have any extra time, please leave a review on Amazon.com, B&N.com, Goodreads.com OR send me a message via Facebook, email, or Twitter and I can personally thank you for reading my novel.

I am so humbled and appreciative that you took the time, and hopefully we will have a long standing book loving relationship.

Thank you! <3 <3 <3

Jessica Florence

Acknowledgements

In my new adventure into the world of writing I'd like to give out HUGE THANK YOU to my cousin Christina for helping me along with writing, editing, for helping me create Fox, and letting me know that it wasn't total disaster.

Thank you to Jeff, Samantha, and Ross for letting me use your names, first or last. Thank you, Mom, even though it was embarrassing as hell to have you read this book, you have been there and I appreciate it. Thank you, Jessica P. and my sister, Katie, for all of your wonderful advice and comments to help me finish my writing.

I definitely couldn't have gotten through writing without listening to music, so thank you, music gods, for inspiration!

Thank you, Cheryl, for your ideas in the beginning and for helping me come up with Candace's character.

To all of my favorite authors who inspired me, Jennifer Armentrout, Alice Clayton, R.K. Lilley, Inara Scott, Laura

Kaye, Rachel Van Dyken, Rick Roirdan, J.K. Rowling. Thank you. Although your books distracted me a lot, they were my greatest inspiration of all. I have always been a reader first and a writer second.

A HUGE thank you to my 9th grade English teacher, Mrs. Daily, I remember your peanut butter and jelly assignment for descriptive writing. I thought of it the whole time I was writing.

Special thanks to my husband, thank you for letting me use your "beach eyes" as inspiration for Darien. Thanks for being there and saying I was amazing for writing.

Thank you, everyone, forsaking a chance and reading the book, and for being supportive!

Jessica <3

About the Author

Jessica Florence, Kaleidoscope of Romance
Author <3 PotterHead <3 Movie Geek Extraordinaire.
Writer of Surviving Valentine. The of The Heart trilogy,
Evergreen,Lights of Scotland Series, and The Final Love
series.
When she's not writing her next invigorating story. You can
find her running her own business, and spending time with
her husband and daughter in southwest Florida.
Jessica loves to interact with her readers

Facebook,Www.JessicaFlorenceAuthor.com

JessicaFlorenceAuthor@gmail.com